The Lonely Ones

A Novel by

Olivia Claire High

Book 3 of the
Island Trilogy

Fireside Publications
Oxford, FL 34484
www.firesidepubs.com

Printed in the United States of America

ISBN: 978-1-935517-41-2

For additional copies of this book, please visit:
http://firesidepubs.com or

Contact the author at:
joeclaire2424@comcast.com

Acknowledgements

A big "Thank You" to my wonderful publisher, Lois Bennett, for all her Guidance.

Dedication

To my Joe,
A very special man.

Chapter One

Riley Hunter squinted at her surroundings through eyelashes beaded with tiny clusters of ice while lacy snowflakes eddied around her, swirling with the whim of the wind. A gleaming world wrapped in a white shroud. Death concealed in beauty. She migrated to Alaska from Hawaii to enjoy the snow, not die in it. Her sojourn today started out happily enough, as she explored this winter wonderland until the sudden storm erupted, catching her unaware.

Riley believed she had headed back to the road towards her car. Now, though, she wandered around long enough to accept that she'd lost her way. She pressed a hand to her coat pocket where her cell phone lay like a silent lump, useless without a signal. She remembered reading about people freezing to death, sometimes within a few feet of their own homes. If those hardy souls who chose to live off the grid, couldn't make it, how could a novice like her expect to survive?

They gave up modern conveniences of towns, civilization, for the peace and quiet of being able to live on their own terms. Personally, she preferred hot water through her fingers and a flushing toilet. Now, even an outhouse with a roof and four walls would look good.

Wind-lashed needles of ice against her face, seeping through the thin layer of her scarf, causing her nose to burn and lips to tingle in the frigid air. Shocked by the cold of her first winter here, she tried to envision herself back in Oahu with soft sand squeezing between her toes, the sound of palm fonds rattling in the breeze, and the scent of plumeria filling the air with the taste of ocean spray on her face. She longed to feel again, her body bathed in the glorious warmth from the sun once more.

The ominous moaning of the storm snapped her back to reality. Ever-increasing layers of snow sucked at her feet creating small craters, as she drudged along. Sane people would be tucked up inside. They'd warm themselves by a fire, sipping a mug of hot cocoa or coffee. The idea that she may be the only living thing existing in this blindingly white world filled her head until she caught a flash of movement out of the corner of her eye. She twisted her body and spotted an animal dressed in its thick winter coat slinking stealthily through the nearby trees.

Riley wiped gloved fingers across her eyes, trying to get a clearer view. She choked out a startled gasp when a large wolf with almond-shaped eyes alert in its narrow-pointed face, peered back. One didn't need to be an animal expert to realize the animal was out in this storm looking for dinner and was pleased to have found today's special here. She felt waves of mounting terror swelling inside her chest, as her heart began to crash against her ribs. She watched the predator creep closer on its' long, spindly legs. Escape flashed into her brain while she did her best to obey the command; yet snow locked her limbs in an unrelenting vise, rendering them motionless.

Riley's head jerked as the sound of crunching footsteps approached from behind. Another figure, larger than the wolf, appeared in her line of vision. A bear? Weren't they supposed to hibernate in winter? She cowered in fear, wondering which one of the beasts would end up feasting on her flesh. The gruesome image brought a high-pitched scream rising in her throat and remain there, as frozen as the rest of her body.

Death. Unexpected. Unplanned. Unwanted. She clutched a hand to her rapidly pounding heart seconds before her eyes rolled back in her head, and she fell into oblivion.

The dark figure fired a warning shot at the wolf, watching it lope away before he scooped Riley into his arms. His snowshoes swished along the ground as his legs wove through flurries of snowflakes that spun through the air, bedecking his clothing in ever-growing flecks of white. He forged determinedly ahead, each step a struggling stride in his quest to reach his destination before the storm became a total white-out. Minutes later, he reached a rustic one room cabin, immediately stepping out of his snowshoes and ducked beneath the doorway. Gently, the stranger lowered her onto the single bed.

She moaned as her body continued to shiver so hard her teeth chattered audibly. Even a novice could see hypothermia could be a very real danger. He wasted no time before he hopped into action. With quick, deft movements, he added more wood to the potbelly stove, coaxing the fire into hot, burning flames. He grabbed a towel from a shelf and gently wiped the snow away from her face, revealing lush auburn brows and lashes beneath the white flakes. He tugged Riley's sodden clothing off piece by piece and began to rub her nude body with brisk strokes.

He tucked her into a sleeping bag before shrugging out of his own outer clothing. His eyes never left Riley while he busied himself draping her wet clothes over a rope line. In time, her body began to shake so violently the man thought he would hear her bones snap at any moment. A resigned sigh escaped him. He reluctantly stripped down to his underwear, settled himself beneath the sleeping bag, and gathered Riley close to him. Hopefully, his body heat would bring the warmth she needed.

He hadn't held a woman in a long time and certainly not a naked one. He gritted his teeth, trying to ignore her delicate curves and the softness of her smooth skin against his flesh. He experienced a few shivers of his own that didn't have anything to do with being cold.

"God help me," he muttered and wiped beads of sweat from his brow as he prepared himself for a very long, very challenging night.

Riley wiggled deeper into the enveloping heat that encased her body. Was this the sunshine she'd thought about or was she dreaming? She didn't care. All she knew was she no longer felt like a popsicle and wild animals weren't getting ready to serve her up as their main course. She kept her eyes closed, wanting to savor every second of feeling warm again until the sound of dishes clinking made her eyelids snap open.

She spotted a man across the room. Room? Riley's gaze wandered around the rough-hewed wooden walls and solid looking plank floor. Not outside in the snow. Not in her apartment. This man must have rescued her and brought her to his humble home. Time to offer her thanks.

Riley cleared her throat.

"Hello," she chirped, as cheerily as she could manage.

He turned to face her; and Riley forgot her words of thanks when she recognized him. Of all the people to save her, why did it have to be a man who didn't like her?

THE LONELY ONES
Olivia Claire High

They'd met several weeks ago when she walked into her boss's office and found him standing with muddy boots on the antique desk while he changed a ceiling light. They exchanged a few sharp barbs. His voice came out as a nice sounding baritone, only spoiled by a nasty disposition.

He walked to the bed with a mug in his hand. Riley sat up and gasped as she realized she was naked. She tugged the edge of the sleeping bag up to her chin.

"A little late for modesty," he raised a brow, "don't you think?"

Ordinarily a voice like his would send a pleasant tingle through her, but not when she was sitting there naked with a man who was almost a stranger.

"Did you take my clothes off?"

"Yes. You weren't in any condition to give me your permission." He thrust the mug toward her. "Here."

She glanced at it with wary eyes. "What's in there?"

"Poison. Drink it and put us both out of our misery. It's coffee. Do you want it or not?"

"Thanks. Are you always in such a bad mood, or is it just me?"

"What makes you think I'm in a bad mood?"

"Oh, I don't know, maybe because you're snapping at me like you did before, Arthur?"

"What did you call me?"

"Don't pretend that's not who you are. I'd recognize your surly attitude anywhere."

"Am I supposed to know you?" Lines creased his forehead, forming into a frown.

"I'm Frances Blair's personal assistant. We met in her office when I yelled at you for . . ."

"Ah. That explains why you looked familiar. So, it's you, Miss Prissy."

"I may be prissy, but I'm also naked, and there's only one single bed."

"Your powers of observation amaze me," his voice deadpan, forehead still wrinkled.

"I want to know if we shared this bed," she demanded, ignoring his sarcasm.

"Yes, it was the only way I could get you to stop shivering. You were half frozen. And before you get the wrong idea, that's all we shared. I'm not into seducing unconscious women."

"Are you saying we were both naked?"

"Not quite. I kept my shorts on. Would you rather I left you in your wet things?" He huffed out an impatient sigh.

"No. I'm sorry. I'm just nervous." She sipped from her mug. "You make good coffee."

"A compliment? Be still my foolish heart."

That made her chuckle.

"Mind if I ask you a question?"

"Depends on what you're asking."

"Your beard has grown quite a bit since we first met. When's the last time you shaved?"

"A while. I'm ugly. The beard keeps me from scaring small animals and little kids."

"Well, all that hair frightened me out there in the snow. I thought you were a bear."

"A bear, huh? I've been called a lot of things, but that's a first." He walked back across the room, turning his back to her again, chuckling softly to himself. "Your oatmeal will be ready in a minute."

"I appreciate your hospitality, but I'll fix my own breakfast as soon as I get home."

"You're not going anywhere in this storm probably for the next few days," he said, pulling back a heavy burlap curtain from one of the small windows, so she could peer outside.

Riley's hand jerked, making coffee slosh around in the mug when she saw snow beating against the glass.

"Oh no! You mean I'm going to be stuck here until the weather clears?"

"I'm looking forward to being with you, too," he drawled.

"I keep saying the wrong thing." Riley's shoulders slumped as she glanced back at him, the corners of her lips turning in a frown, "I'm sorry. I haven't even thanked you for saving my life."

"Forget it. I didn't do anything that anyone else wouldn't have done."

"Well, I really am grateful. Um... how do you contact people in case of an emergency?"

"I don't. I prefer not to have people bug me. That's why I live out here on my own."

"Isn't it risky? What if you get sick, or have an accident? Who would take care of you?"

"Either I take care of myself, or I suffer the consequences."

"That seems like a very dangerous way of looking at things to me."

"Well, I'm not you."

"I bet a woman made you shut yourself away. What's the matter, did she break your heart?"

Riley realized she must have hit a nerve when the spoon in his hand clattered to the counter and she saw his back muscles bunch beneath the material of his shirt. He waited a few seconds before he brought her oatmeal, long enough to regain control of himself, and took her empty mug back to the counter without a word. She gnawed her bottom lip. Maybe he loved a woman who died.

"What's your last name?" she asked, hoping to redeem herself.

"Does it matter?"

"I guess not, but now I'm wondering if it's something embarrassing like Weinerpickle."

"You seem to have a warped sense of humor."

"My bad." She finished her oatmeal, licking the last bit off her bottom lip with the tip of her tongue and shifting awkwardly. "I hate to ruin all this wonderful ambiance, but I'm afraid I have to use the outhouse."

"I figured you would. I laid out some of my stuff on the chair since your clothes are still wet. Roll up the cuffs. Gonna have to wear your own boots, but I'll give you a pair of my socks."

"Thanks..." Riley said, waiting for him to move. When he didn't, she knew she'd have to say more. "Mind turning around, so I can get out of bed?"

"Seems kind of a waste of time considering I've already seen you naked."

She wrinkled her nose at him.

"Thanks for the reminder. I happened to be in La La Land then and didn't know you were looking, but now I do. At least I'll have the illusion of privacy." He still hadn't budged an inch. "Are you going to turn around or not?"

"Turning now, ma'am," he said in a crisp voice while demonstrating a snappy salute.

She began to quickly dress before he could change his mind and look back. "Nice, you deserve a twenty-one guns salute."

"Too noisy."

"Not necessarily. I meant a silent one."

"There's no such thing."

"There is, actually. Have you ever heard of the Arizona Memorial on Oahu?"

8

"What American hasn't?"

"Well, there are twenty-one openings," she went on, ignoring his tone, "seven on each side, and seven on top. They are meant to represent a perpetual silent salute."

"I never knew that, but it seems a fitting tribute. Dressed yet?"

"I'm just doing up the last button. Okay, you can turn around now. How do I look?"

"Like someone playing dress up in clothes several sizes too big. Let's do this. Be sure you stay close to me. I don't think either of us would want to have you get lost again."

"Definitely not. I understand I'm an uninvited intruder into your life here. But I want you to know I promise I will do whatever you say to try and make the best of our situation."

His eyes traveled the length of her body.

"You may want to be careful what you promise."

Sharing personal space in a one room cabin without bumping into each other presented a challenge for a man used to living on his own. Riley's smile and friendly chatter filled what traditionally were long, lonely hours. He encouraged her to give him glimpses of her life but gave scant details himself. She went to great lengths to describe her years growing up on Oahu, including snorkeling, learning to surf, beach picnics, and midnight swims with friends in secret coves. She told him she spent years working at her father's bakery for a job. He was especially interested in what made her move to Alaska and almost regretted his curiosity when she explained her father died and she thought it would be a good change after looking at friends' photos from a vacation here.

THE LONELY ONES
Olivia Claire High

He couldn't resist taking her in front of the cabin when she revealed she always wanted to build a snowman. The wind clawed at them with icy fingers while the snow blanketed their clothes until they looked like snow creatures. But every goose bump they endured ended up being small payment when Riley sat by the window later smiling and staring at their creation. It reminded him of an excited child on Christmas morning.

His shirt came down passed her knees and his socks snaked up her legs, providing plenty of cover, but he had a difficult time blocking out how she looked without clothes. He tried not to think about that and avoided getting too close to her as much as possible, especially at night. He insisted she have the bed while he used a sleeping bag on the floor.

Once when she cried out in her sleep, he reached out to comfort her, then stopped, afraid he might be tempted to offer more than she wanted. His body ached with need, tormented by visions of soft, creamy flesh, while he tossed and turned in his sleeping bag.

But that was about to change.

Chapter Two

Hours turned into days; and they began to snip at each other for the most minor of offenses. He tried to explain cabin fever to Riley, but he knew better. They happened to be two healthy people thrown into close quarters who were becoming sexually attracted to each other.

"When is this storm ever going to end?" Riley grumbled.

"A day or two."

"That's what you keep saying. I don't know how you stand being cooped up here. Do you want to know what I think the real reason is why you stay isolated?"

"No."

"Well, I'm going to tell you anyway. I think you stay here because you're afraid if you leave you will have to involve yourself in society and interact with people."

"I don't need to be around people to make me happy."

"What's that supposed to mean?" Riley put her hands on her hips. "Are you saying I need special entertainment?"

"Well, you are the one who is doing all the complaining."

"That does it! I've had enough of you mocking me. You may want to live like a hermit, but I prefer to be around civilized people." She grabbed her coat off a hook and stomped to the door.

"Just where the hell do you think you're going?"

"Out!" She shouted before running outside into the relentlessly swirling snow.

"Damn it!" He yanked on a coat and ducked his head out the door to stop her. Riley fought to be free when he seized her by the arms. She struggled in his grip until she ended up making them both lose their balance and fall onto the snow where she lay pinned beneath him.

"Let me go!" she shouted, pushing against his chest.

"Stop this idiocy right now and get your butt back inside."

"I'd rather stay out here than have to spend another minute with you in that cabin."

"You're going to freeze if you stay out here."

"I don't care! Now get off me you . . . you big ape."

"You will care when your fingers turn black and your face looks like raw hamburger."

Riley punched his shoulders. He swore, locked both her wrists in one hand, steadied her chin with the other, and crushed his mouth to her lips. She ceased struggling, beginning to kiss him back. He pulled away and jumped to his feet, taking her hand and tugging her to the cabin.

He closed the door and ran a hand around his neck.

"I shouldn't have kissed you. I'm sorry."

"I'm not. I'd like more." She touched a fingertip to her lips. "I want you to make love to me."

"Absolutely not." He tossed his coat on a chair, shaking his head in disbelief.

"Why? You've seen me naked. Is it because you find my body repulsive?"

"Don't be stupid."

"You said you're sorry you kissed me. Does that mean you don't like women?"

"I'm a heterosexual male supposedly in my sexual prime. What do you think?"

"Then why are you refusing me?" Riley asked, shrugging out of her own coat.

"Because you deserve someone besides a broken-down bum like me."

"I'm not asking for tomorrow."

The problem was he did want tomorrow and a lot longer than that. She looked so inviting that it made him ache more than ever to have her. He had two choices. He could either go outside and roll naked in the snow to douse his rising libido or take Riley to bed and bury himself in her.

"Want to change your mind?" She began to unbutton her shirt giving him a glimpse of skin.

Oh, yeah. He was probably going to regret it, but he'd worry about that later. They stumbled onto the bed together. Hands tore at clothing. Hearts pounded. Breaths came in excited pants, as he surged forward overcome by his own uncontrollable passion. He groaned out his release and knew he ended far too quickly for her. He began to apologize again.

"That's okay," she said, stroking his cheek. "I guess you've been storing up, huh?"

"It sure as hell is not okay. I left you with nothing while I satisfied myself. Give me a few moments to recover and I'll make it better. Round one was for me. Round two will be yours."

This time when he wrapped his arms around her, the sweetness of his mouth rubbing over her lips made Riley shiver in anticipation. He proved with every touch, every movement the incredible skills he possessed as a lover. Much later, she lay beneath him smiling with the satisfaction of a woman who knew she had just been thoroughly sated.

She savored the thought of spending the night with him in bed seconds before his weight lifted off her.

Confused, she sat up and stared as he pulled on his clothes.

"What are you doing?"

"Go to sleep, Riley."

"I thought we were going to spend the night together."

"You said you weren't going to ask for tomorrow. I'm holding you to that."

"Oh, right. Sorry. I guess I forgot the rules there for a moment." She snapped back at him. Getting the words to pass the lump lodged in her throat took effort. Rolling over to hide her expression was the only way she could conceal her sense of burning humiliation.

Riley's nostrils twitched at the aroma of coffee. She sat up and stretched her arms above her head, revealing her naked breasts.

"Good morning."

"Get dressed," a muscle jumped in his cheek, as he shoved a mug into her hands seconds before he turned away. "The storm has passed. You'll finally get your wish to leave."

"I don't mind it so much now that we made love. Don't you want me?"

"Too much, but it ends here and now. I gave into a moment of weakness and allowed my physical needs to cloud my judgment. I'd rather you didn't make it out to be more than it was."

His indifference hurt. But Riley didn't want to leave here without having her say.

"Making love with you was one of the most beautiful experiences of my life. I'm sorry I asked for more. No wonder you're angry with me."

"I'm angry with myself. Now please get dressed. I'd like to leave as soon as possible."

"Don't let the door hit me in the butt on the way out," she muttered with as much dignity as she could manage. "Can't wait to get rid of me, eh?"

"It's time that you should go back. Mrs. Blair must be concerned over you being gone this long."

"No, she won't. She told us all to take a week off while she had the office repainted."

"I had no idea she planned on doing that."

"Spur of the moment decisions don't come with a plan." Riley drank coffee while he went outside to get things ready. "How do I respond to you at work?" she asked when he returned.

"I'm not going back there."

"I won't mention about us if that will get you fired." She set the mug aside with great care.

"Thank you for your concern, but I will find a job at another site."

She wondered if he wanted to dismiss her from his life because of the mystery woman she teased him about, the one that left him silent to her taunts. But whatever the reason, he made it clear he didn't need to see her again.

Riley found out Arthur left for the Anchorage site. She struggled to concentrate on her job when memories of their time in the cabin disrupted all other thoughts. She lied to her boss, saying she laid around at home during the break. There was no need to give Frances the wrong impression by sharing how she shacked up with a man she barely knew. Frances hired her when she didn't have any experience. Her friendship meant everything to Riley, as did her respect; she refused to consider losing it. After all, she was having enough trouble respecting herself.

A wave of empathy swept over her as she recalled the story Frances shared one day when helping Riley to become familiar with the company's beginnings. It seemed that Frances struggled with her own issues, too. She wasn't just Riley's boss but was the granddaughter of the company's founder, Ernest Liam King, who started out right here in Juneau many years ago.

E. L. King began by using his own initials to form an acronym, then used those same letters to create the name for his new company, *ELK,* a company specializing in outdoor clothing and camping equipment with stores in several cities scattered throughout Alaska. Riley worked at the Juneau site.

Earnest retired long before Riley arrived and turned the helm over to his son Edward Liam King. Edward didn't have his father's business sense and nearly brought the company to ruin with his poor investments and lavish lifestyle. Earnest eventually fired Edward and insisted Frances take charge, making her balance work with a busy home life that included eight-year-old twin boys.

Riley heard Frances say she wished her brother would take her place, but he preferred to stay in the field, testing out the new equipment. Riley thought he sounded selfish, but what did she know, since she'd never met the man?

Later, Riley tapped on the office door, peeking around the corner. Frances gestured for her to come in.

"I brought the data you wanted. Should I send a copy to your husband's office?"

"No. I'm just curious about a few things. He might think I'm meddling in the company's accounting. You know how it is. Male pride. Wouldn't sit too well with him being the accountant."

"And speaking of that, your father just called again. Did you want me to cancel tomorrow's lunch date with him? If so, what reason would you like to use this time?"

Frances pinched the bridge of her nose with her thumb and forefinger.

"I had hoped he would give up. I suppose I'll have to go. I'll call him myself."

"He said to tell you he would pick you up here, and he's bringing Harper. Is that his dog?" Riley asked quizzically.

Frances let out a peal of laughter. "I wish! Harper is just the latest floozy he's charming these days. But he won't be wasting any of that charm on me for making him wait. A peace offering may mollify him. Sorry to ask, but could you pick up something? I'm too busy now."

"I'll do my best. Can you give me an idea what he might like?"

"Anything, as long as it's expensive and flashy. Charge it to the office account. He doesn't deserve anything with the generous monthly allowance he gets for doing nothing, and the only reason he wants this lunch is to badger me into asking my grandfather to give him more."

Her phone rang as soon as Riley left. Frances glanced at the screen and took the call.

"Are you at the house? Have you seen Grandpa?"

"Yeah. I barely had my coat off before he started going on about me returning to the office."

"He's not the only one. You know I could use your help around here."

"God, don't you start, too. I can't stand the idea of going back even if I thought I could."

"Will you at least stay longer this time? The boys miss you and that goes double for me."

"I miss you guys too. I'll try to hang around for a while."

"Good. Besides wanting to see you, I have a business glitch I need to talk to you about."

"Okay, as long as it doesn't have anything to do with the accident," he warned.

"You know me better than that. I hate the thought just as much as you do. You nearly died and as if that wasn't bad enough, it nearly drove you to the edge of insanity."

"What makes you think I'm sane now?" he said and cut the connection.

A quick rush of tears filled her eyes. She wished with all her heart she could make his pain go away but how could a person save someone who believed they were beyond saving?

Chapter Three

Slumped at her desk twiddling her pen, Riley contemplated on what to buy for Edward King. She already scratched lines through a couple items. What would take the edge off his temper before he met with Frances, short of wrapping up money for him? He clearly resented his family for voting him out after his disastrous reign when he tried to head the company. Venting his sour attitude on Frances seemed like a lousy way to treat his own daughter.

He reminded Riley of a spoiled child throwing tantrums. Edward lost the status of being a businessman in charge of a very successful company because of his ineptness. One day he was Mr. Big Shot, sauntering around town socializing with other powerful men until his father booted him out. Now, he was just another irresponsible guy living off his family's hard-earned money.

Edward received a generous stipend to live on, so he obviously still enjoyed a somewhat privileged lifestyle. Wine, women, and song, as the old saying went. Why wasn't that enough? A man who already had too much and demanded more could be hard to buy for. Riley continued to jot down ideas until she suddenly realized what the gift could be. She was just thinking about wine, so why not buy some Alaskan wine and have the bottles gift wrapped in a fancy box.

Riley was reminded of something she once read that Napoleon Bonaparte said:

"In victory, you deserve champagne, in defeat, you need it."

Hopefully, it would appease Edward enough to keep him from chastising Frances before she ended up having heartburn at lunch. Riley thought about her own father. A different man entirely compared to Edward. Time and miles hadn't lessened her sorrow at his death, especially when she went into one of the local bakeries here. The aroma of freshly baked goods tantalized her senses while stirring up memories of watching him whipping up his masterpieces.

Some artists used paint brushes. Her dad used flour and a lot of other ingredients for his creations.

Riley once explained to Frances she preferred to work in a different environment rather than be reminded every day of how her father devoted his life to his business. She appreciated Frances understanding her feelings. Yet another reason Riley thought of her not only as her boss, but also as a friend. She had experienced firsthand the importance of friendship, especially when it meant the difference between life and death.

Long ago, she aided her friend Tessa back home to escape a killer. Thank God, the terrifying situation ended up being resolved when the killer was caught. But Riley never forgot how it felt to know she held the fate of her friend in her hands.

Did Frances think because she was the only female in the family that she was responsible for making sure they all lived happy lives? Sometimes, Riley thought she detected an aura of sadness about her boss. Was it because she had too much stress in her life, or was there something more bothering her? Every family had their secrets.

Some just happened to be more heartbreaking than others.

Riley hoped this wasn't the case.

Ernest looked down his long nose at the others sitting at the dining table; there were Frances and her husband Wayne, with their twin sons Tyson and Tyler who sat next to Erik King. The old man's eyes remained focused on Erik during most of the dinner as he studied his grandson. But he diverted his attention to the children now, frowning at the food left on their plates.

"You two going to eat or continue making a mess?" he demanded.

Forks clattered onto their plates and small hands quickly ducked beneath the table. Wayne answered.

"They don't care for stewed tomatoes," Wayne answered for his sons.

"Then why did you serve them some?"

"I wanted to see if they changed their minds."

"Bah! You ate the food you were given when I was their age whether you liked it or not."

Frances' fingers tightened on her own fork before she sent the children a reassuring smile.

"Go play in your room. I'll be up in a little while to help you get ready for your bath."

They scrambled off their chairs and ran from the room before tempers could escalate further.

"How do you expect them to grow up to be tough if you mollycoddle them so much?" Ernest's bushy eyebrows pinched together.

"Forcing them to eat something they don't like isn't mollycoddling them, Grandpa."

Erik stood up, taking advantage of Ernest focusing on Frances, but Ernest immediately shifted his attention back to him.

"Where do you think you're going?" he growled, heightening the tension in the room.

"I thought I'd go spend some time with the boys."

"You have more important things to do than babysit kids. I told you we need to talk."

"Not tonight, Grandpa." Erik shook his head. "I'm tired, and I just want to relax."

"What you have to be tired about I don't know. Fine, run off, but make no mistake we will have our conversation before you leave this house again."

Ernest took a deep swallow from his wineglass, scowling as Erik quitted the room.

"He looks worse than the last time he was here. I've given him enough time to lick his wounds. When the devil will he stop behaving like a hermit and remember who he is? He needs to come back here where he belongs."

"Perhaps he doesn't feel like he *does* belong here now," Frances answered in a quiet voice.

"Nonsense! This is his home, damn it."

She stood up and began to gather dirty dishes, tidying up.

"No, Grandpa, it hasn't been for a long time."

Erik's long legs sprawled out in front of him as he sat on the floor with his nephews, their eyes locked on the television screen. He had no idea what program had them so riveted. Not that he didn't care; he came here to enjoy their uncomplicated company. His grandfather had watched him all through dinner just like they watched their show, waiting for the right moment to demand an audience. The lecture was always about when he planned on coming back here to live. When was he going to take his rightful place in the company?

He truly felt for his grandfather. The man worked so hard to create the business only to be rewarded with his own son nearly ruining everything. Erik didn't dare offer to be the fixer his grandfather wanted. He couldn't, not when the very thought made him break out in a sweat. He dealt with the anxieties that held him back every day, grinding away at his confidence. His own father's only excuse turned out to be he was a natural screw up. Perhaps that made him sound like a crappy son, but no one would ever describe Edward as a devoted dad.

Born with the proverbial silver spoon in his mouth, Edward nearly choked on it. His life of privilege fed into years of debauchery, chasing away Erik's mother when he was very young, leaving him without many memories of her. There had been no secret of the fact Ernest wanted heirs, so Edward had married simply to keep his place in the old man's will. A picture of his mother was all Erik had to know what she looked like. A precious gift from Frances. In it, her ponytail and simple cotton dress made her look quite young and vulnerable. Most assuredly, not someone who would be able to take on the likes of his father.

Had she loved him?

Perhaps.

Did he feel as deeply for her?

Doubtful.

Frances made him promise not to tell their father about the photo and he never did. His elder by five years, she had always been the person he gravitated to the most. Today, she still was his most trusted ally. She and the twins were the only reason he ever bothered to come back here. The constant nagging wasn't an incentive and he didn't share a particularly close relationship with his brother-in-law.

Strange, given they met in college. Frances enrolled in some graduate courses and Erik introduced them. He hadn't spent a lot of time with Wayne, learning later that Frances hung out with him a lot more. So much so, when she announced they were going to be married. Erik recalled having mixed feelings about that; in the end, he kept his thoughts to himself.

Frances talked Ernest into hiring Wayne as the company's accountant, always wanting Erik to be closer with Wayne. Unfortunately, they didn't have much in common. Erik preferred the outdoors, while her husband was more of an inside person. Once, he tried by taking his brother-in-law camping. The man couldn't even figure out how to set up a simple pup tent. He also didn't have any interest in hunting, fishing, or rafting. Not too great when the family had made their fortune selling the gear for it. There came a point where no amount of coaching was going to turn Wayne into an outdoorsman. In the end, the family left him to his numbers.

A fight broke out over the remote, interrupting Erik's thoughts. He grabbed it and tossed it aside, bringing loud yelps of protest. No problem. He knew how to stop their whining.

"Looks like you guys have put on a little muscle since I was here last. Are you up for a little wrestling to show me what you've got?"

Protests instantly turned to shouts of joy as both boys jumped on Erik and the three of them were soon rolling around on the floor.

When Frances came down the hall, she heard their laughter. She peeked around the corner of the door and smiled at the sight. The boys loved to wrestle, and she often wished Wayne would indulge them. But he didn't care for roughhousing as he called it. She loved seeing how much fun the children were having. It did her heart good to hear Erik laughing too. She stood there and indulged herself, watching for another minute before she came into full view and cleared her throat.

"The bath is ready if you two monkeys are finished hugging your uncle."

"Hugging?" Tyson snorted in disgust. "Mom, we're wrestling. Hugging is for girls."

"Yeah, girls," Tyler chimed in, ever the faithful brother.

"Well, how about you wrestle yourselves down to the bathroom? And don't forget to put your dirty clothes in the hamper. I'll be there in a few minutes."

"We'll have a rematch later," Erik promised when they began to pout.

She waited until her sons left the room before she motioned Erik to one of the single beds. She sat beside him and reached over to push a wave of hair away from his eyes.

"You need a haircut."

"I need a lot of things."

"Don't we all? Dad wants to go to lunch tomorrow. Will you join us?"

"I'd rather shave using a dry razor, running in place, and singing the National Anthem."

"I'll take that as a no, then."

"Come on, Fran." He reached over and took hold of her hand. "You know he doesn't want to see me. All we would do is end up trading nasty jibes, just giving you indigestion if I went."

"I suppose it would be too much to ask if we behaved like a normal family."

"I have no idea what a normal family entails and neither do you, so there's no sense wishing for what we don't understand." He let go of her hand. "Are you here to tell me about the glitch?"

"Yes." She reached into the pocket of her slacks and handed him a couple sheets of folded paper. "I'd like you to look at these. Keep them out of sight until you get to your room. I made some notes of my own and would like to hear your opinion."

He shoved the papers in his shirt pocket.

"Can you give me a hint what it's about?"

"I started receiving calls from angry customers and things just don't add up for me."

"What things?"

"Orders supposedly lost. Or never placed but paid for. Missing stock from the warehouse. There were business trips I didn't know about and donations to charities Wayne never mentioned too."

"This kind of thing is bound to happen in a company as large as Elk. I'm sure Wayne knows, but doesn't want to bother you. You can always dig deeper if it has you this worked up."

"I'm working on that, but I have to do it without him finding out. He hates anything that might remotely seem like I'm criticizing his bookkeeping. . . Or anything else for that matter."

"I'm getting the vibe this isn't just about work. Is everything okay between you two?"

She pressed her lips together for a moment.

"I don't know. Sometimes I get the feeling . . ."

Wayne's voice interrupted calling from the bathroom.

"Frances, you'd better come in here. Your sons have splashed water all over the bathroom floor as usual."

"I notice they're my sons when they've done something Wayne doesn't like." She sighed. "Duty calls." She walked to the door and stopped. "Please don't forget to look at those papers."

"I won't, and try not to worry so much." Erik patted his shirt pocket.

"It seems like worry has become my middle name," she said, hurrying from the room.

Wayne appeared a minute later.

"I keep telling and telling your sister not to leave those two alone at bath time because they usually end up making a mess."

"They're just little kids. Cut them some slack. That's what they do."

"Try telling that to your grandfather. *His* house so we have to abide by *his* rules."

"Get your own place then. You all would be happier if the episode at dinner was usual."

"I would much rather move out, but Frances refuses to leave him here on his own."

Erik winced, knowing this was another responsibility he'd put on his sister.

"I'm sorry. I know it would make things a lot easier if I just came back and stayed with him instead."

"I didn't come in here to put a guilt trip on you. Frances said you promised to stay longer this time so your grandfather wanted me to ask if you would consider coming to the office, just for a couple days," he quickly tagged on at the end.

"So much for no guilt trip."

"I'm sorry. It wasn't my idea to put that kind of pressure on you, but Ernest . . ."

"Sent you in here to work on me?"

Wayne's hands fluttered in the air signaling denial. "No, no, it wasn't like that. He just thought I could suggest the idea to you, since I was coming in here anyway. You didn't give him much chance to ask you at dinner. Don't you ever think about coming back?"

"Every damn day. But that particular mountain never gets any easier to climb. You can tell my grandfather that I'll go back when I'm ready. Not before."

"I think it would be better if you told him yourself."

"Probably. Not that it will do any good."

"It's good to have you here if only for a while. It means a lot to Frances." Wayne walked to the door. "I hope you sleep well. Warning though, the boys are early risers."

"There are a lot of worse things to wake up to than a couple of noisy kids."

"I suppose that would depend on a person's level of tolerance. Goodnight, Erik."

Chapter Four

Erik's eyes blinked. Fighting the darkness. Fighting sleep. Fighting his fears. Who needed heart pounding images that invaded dreams and left him waking soaked in sweat? The thought he would be better off putting a gun to his head when the nightmares became too intense used to seem like a good idea. But thinking of Frances standing by a gaping hole, staring down at his coffin, would intrude and force him to endure his demons.

Not that him being alive was doing her much good. The longer he stayed away, the more strain he put on her. She carried the burden of too many responsibilities, and he was one of them. She wouldn't have to be in this position if he returned to work.

Erik rubbed circles over his abdomen trying to relieve the tense muscles, thinking about his last days at the office. A lone man in an arena with people staring at him, pointing fingers, and speculating.

He uttered an angry curse. Enough of this self-torture. He leaned over, turned on the bedside lamp, and swung his legs over the edge of the bed. Scanning the room, seeking a distraction, he stopped when he spotted his shirt hanging over a chair. He wasn't particularly interested in anything to do with the family business, but what the hell else did he have to do?

He padded, barefoot, to the garment and drew out Frances's papers. A quick perusal didn't send up any major red flags. Hopefully, she wouldn't find anything more worth digging into because then his sister really would expect him to go back to running the company.

He cursed his selfishness and shoved the papers back. The inability to get on with his life left him weak with shame and filled to the brim with disgust. It wasn't that he was lazy, more about the type of work he preferred these days. He'd much rather chop wood than sit behind a desk, staring at a computer screen. He did promise Fran that he would stay for a while, yet their grandfather's lectures alone were enough to make him regret that decision.

God, he did not want to be here. Sad, considering this was the house he grew up in. His rare visits weren't exactly happy family reunions. There always seemed to be an undercurrent of tension in the house despite his sister's best efforts to create the normal family she so desperately craved.

Frances. God bless her. She deserved a medal for never giving up on him even when he rewarded that allegiance by ignoring her cries for help. Running away hadn't done anything to resolve his issues. Still, he continued to try and shut out the world. The world didn't care. It kept knocking at his door. He grounded his palms into his eyes now, wondering just what it would take to make him be the man his sister believed him to be.

The man that he once was . . . before he fell apart.

Riley twirled in front of her mirror and pressed both hands against her flat abdomen. Butterflies of nervous excitement fluttered there. She stuck her leg out from the slit in her long gown and stared at the high heeled sandal. Wearing flip flops back home and now low-heeled shoes and sturdy boots hadn't prepared her for the challenge of such a drastic change in footwear. She had practiced several times today alone, walking in her new shoes, yet still didn't feel quite as graceful as the models and movie stars looked on television.

She wanted to look nice not only for herself, but for Frances as well. This was the first time her boss would be letting the important people in town officially meet her assistant. Riley hoped she would make a good show of herself, knowing first impressions were often something that stayed in peoples' minds even after you walked away.

This event celebrated Ernest King's birthday. He gave two major parties a year according to his granddaughter; one during the Christmas holidays, and another in the summer for his birthday. Both were formal affairs. ELK employees were invited and expected to dress accordingly, so she guided Riley and even made sure she had a date for the event.

Frances had been insisting that Riley needed to have more of a social life after watching her go out by herself for months. Finally, she introduced Riley to Harve, a young man who worked in the warehouse. They had already gone on a few dates, but nothing as fancy as this party promised to be.

The muscles in her throat tightened for a moment. The urge to cry rose strong, but Riley forced the sadness away, knowing her father wouldn't want her to be upset. This was supposed to be a night of celebration, not tears. A knock at the door made her grab her evening bag and a lacey stole. She hurried into the living room and opened the door to Harve.

"Wow, you look great," he gasped in greeting.

"Thanks. You look very handsome yourself. Haven't seen you in a suit before."

"And you wouldn't if I had my choice." He tugged awkwardly at the sleeve of his jacket. "I borrowed the suit from my uncle, but the shirt and tie are mine. Seems like a lot of fuss to have to dress up like this." he shrugged, glancing back at her, "Ready to go?"

"I want your opinion first." She held up her wrap. "I really would like to use this stole instead of my coat, but I'll probably be too cold. Should I go vanity or practicality?"

He scratched his head.

"Women's clothing is not my thing, but if you want to wear the stole I can drop you off at the door and you can go inside while I park. Don't need to be worried about the cold there. The place will be packed with people and it can get pretty darn warm. Besides, you probably don't want to walk too far in those anyway," he said pointing to her shoes.

"Vanity again. How did you know?"

"My mom has shoes she calls going out to dinner shoes where she can sit most of the time because they look good but are too uncomfortable to do anything else."

"Your mother is a wise lady. Alright, lead the way." Riley stopped when Harve led her to an SUV a few minutes later. "What happened to your truck? Did you buy this since our last date?"

"I wish, but not on my salary. It's my dad's. He said I should have a better vehicle than my old truck for this party. You'd think we were going to meet royalty the way everyone carries on."

"How will your parents get to the party?" Riley asked, carefully lifting the hem of her dress before sliding into the passenger seat.

"Only ELK employees and big shot people in business are guests. My parents aren't either."

"I didn't know that. I just assumed they worked for the Kings."

"There's a lot of things you don't know about me, but I'd like to get to know you better."

Riley looked down at her lap wondering how best to reply to his comment. Harve might have wanted a deeper relationship between them. But how could she give herself to a boy when she'd already been possessed by a man?

"Tell me about this party. The ladies in the office raved about it."

A driver pulled in front of him, providing the distraction Riley needed.

"Well, this is only my second time. Old man King doesn't spare expenses on food and booze. My hangover last year lasted two days and I'll probably have one as bad after tonight. But it's only a couple times a year. Probably should have warned you that we'll have to take a cab home if I do get too soused. That okay?"

"Sounds delightful."

Riley stood at the entry to the beautiful Victorian mansion, admiring the stain glass windows, rich mahogany wall paneling, and intricate inlaid floor design. The Kings may not be royalty, but this was the closest thing to a castle she'd ever visited. She moved further inside, drawn by the sound of music in the grand ballroom. Men and women clad in their formal wear hovered like sparkling moths beneath the two dazzling crystal chandeliers.

She peered through the crowd hoping to spot one of her co-workers when a figure came rushing up to her in a whirl of mauve taffeta.

"I've been watching for you." Frances exclaimed, "Let me have a look. Your dress is lovely. The shade of yellow goes with your hair perfectly."

"Thank you. I love yours too."

Frances ran a hand down one hip. "Quite a difference from our usual work attire, isn't it?" She looked over Riley's shoulder. "Where's Harve? Do not tell me he stood you up."

"Oh no, he let me off while he parks the car. I have a feeling he'll have trouble finding me with so many people around. I probably should wait for him right here."

"It's most certainly going to take a while to find a parking spot. That gives us time." She surprised Riley by grabbing her by the hand, ignoring her protests, and started weaving their way through the packed room, clearly a woman on a mission.

The high heeled shoes nearly sent Riley stumbling as she did her best to keep up.

"Time for what? Where are you taking me?"

"I want you to meet someone very special."

"All right, but I hope Harve won't be upset that I took off without him."

"Don't worry, he knows you're here and he'll find you. What I have in mind can't wait."

Frances's flushed cheeks and bright smile gave her an air of excitement that Riley had never noticed about her employer before. She wondered if it was because of the party, or this special person she seemed so anxious to have her meet. Frances smiled and gave brief comments to people while they wound their way through the crowd, but she didn't allow anyone to delay her for more than a few seconds.

Finally, they came to a halt and Frances pointed to a man standing with his back to them. "Good, he's where I left him. I had to move fast before he went to another room and I end up spending half the night trying to get you two together."

Riley made a fast study of the man. The cut of his tuxedo fit his tall frame and broad shoulders to perfection, making her believe the clothes were probably tailormade. His straight raven black hair had just enough length that she bet any woman would be tempted to run their fingers through the thick waves . . . including her, much to her surprise.

Frances tapped him on his shoulder. He excused himself from the people he was talking to. Riley readied her smile. Mustn't disappoint Frances. Her special person turned to face them.

And the bottom dropped out of Riley's world.

"I'd like you to meet my brother Erik King," Frances said, making the introductions with just enough flourish to make it sound as though he might be the royalty Harve joked about. "Erik, this is Riley Hunter, the wonderful assistant I've been bragging to you about."

He extended his hand. Somewhere in her dazed mind, Riley's brain managed to signal that she needed to reach out to accept his handshake. His long fingers engulfed her hand, sending a tingling sensation surging through her entire body.

"Ms. Hunter, what a pleasure to finally meet you."

She sucked in her breath. She knew that voice in every fiber of her being. Hadn't she been haunted by the memory of that deep baritone for weeks and weeks?

Frances laughed and waved a hand in front of Riley. "Aren't you going to say anything?"

"Sorry, I thought I did. How do you do, Mr. King?" She tugged her hand from his grasp, embarrassment deepening the color beneath her makeup.

"Ms. Hunter. Mr. King. So formal," Frances scoffed. "Come on now, I want you two to be friends." She patted Riley on the arm. "Don't feel bad about your reaction. This handsome devil has that effect on just about any woman he meets."

His deep chuckle sent another unsettling zing right down to Riley's toes.

"Fran, you'll frighten the poor girl telling her things like that."

"Well, it's true. Oh, don't forget it's your turn to give the birthday toast this year."

"How can I forget when you keep reminding me every five minutes?" He touched her cheek.

"Relax, the party will be another success thanks to your careful planning and attention to detail."

"I hope so. I need to make another run to the kitchen to check on the catering staff. It looked like the canapes were running low when I came through the room. You two get acquainted."

Riley almost took a step after her wishing she could flee as easily. She'd even offer to wash dishes in the kitchen if she thought it would get her out of her situation. It was her heart. The mad hammering left her worried she might faint if it didn't slow down.

"My sister tells me you are from Hawaii."

His tone was friendly enough, but his eyes made her nervous. In fact, everything about this man put her on edge. She sensed a commanding aura about him that radiated a potent combination of power and sexiness.

"Yes," Riley could barely get the word passed her parched throat and nearly breathed out a sigh of relief when she saw Harve hovering nearby. "My date is probably looking for me. It was nice meeting you, Mr. King. Maybe, um, we'll see each other at your grandfather's Christmas party."

"Oh, I'm sure we'll be seeing each other much sooner than that, Ms. Hunter."

God, she hoped not! Riley hurried away and grabbed a glass of champagne off a tray from a passing waiter. She rarely drank alcohol, but right now she needed help to calm her nerves. The drink rushed down her throat and she coughed when the bubbles tickled her nose. She dared a glance over her shoulder and saw Erik King watching her with a gaze as disturbing as the man himself. A shiver shimmied up her spine, as she hurried toward Harve. She needed some fresh air and fast.

Either she was losing her mind, or Erik King and Arthur were one and the same man.

Chapter Five

Sleep alluded Riley for most of the weekend. *How was she supposed to pretend the strange encounter at the party hadn't happened?* She avoided being anywhere near Erik after their brief meeting. In fact, she especially made it a point to dodge Frances knowing how important that introduction had been to her. Riley dreaded going to work this morning, fearing her boss might ask for details on how she got along with the precious brother. Maybe she could sidetrack questions by using the truth that Harve showed up not long after.

Harve did end up getting drunk. Nevertheless, he saw her safely home in a taxi and called the next day to apologize. She assured him she wasn't angry. The poor guy's hangover sounded like punishment enough. Her own headache had nothing to do with alcohol and everything to do with her meeting Erik King. The touch of his hand, the sound of his voice, everything about him caused her to suffer some serious sensory overload, if all that tingling going on in her body had anything to say about the encounter.

Riley drove to work, and after walking into the office, shoved her purse into a drawer only to slam it shut in the next instant. From the corner of her eye, she noticed one of the ladies looking up and giving her a sympathetic smile.

"You look almost as bad as I feel. I promise myself every year I won't drink too much champagne, but it's just too tempting and tastes so darn good."

"I do not have a hangover," Riley snapped, hanging her coat on the back of her chair.

"Well, excuse me!" the woman, snipped back, raising her eyebrows while trying to hide a smile.

"I'm sorry. I didn't mean to be rude. I only had one glass of champagne, but I think I must have eaten too much rich food because I've had an upset stomach all weekend," she lied.

"That can happen if you're not used to it. I have something to help in my purse. . ."

"Thank you, but I've already taken something. Has Mrs. Blair been in her office long?"

"Not long at all. You're supposed to go in, and you don't have to bother knocking."

Riley frowned. Did she detect an odd note in the woman's voice? Perhaps she was still miffed at her earlier rudeness. She almost offered another apology before she decided it best to let the subject drop. Opening the door to Frances' office, she knew immediately why her co-worker sounded so strange.

Erik King stood at the big window, not Frances Blair.

He turned to greet her with a smile.

"Good morning."

"What are you doing here?" she blurted out, gripping the doorknob tightly.

"I do believe I said we would be seeing each other soon. Please close the door."

"Where is Mrs. Blair?" She did as he asked and stood there, her body stiff with uncertainty.

"She left this morning for a well-deserved vacation with her family." He walked over to a counter, lifting a glass coffeepot. "Would you like some?"

"What are you doing?" she demanded. Accusation filled her eyes.

He cocked a brow.

"Offering you coffee."

"Stop it! You know very well I'm not talking about coffee. I know who you really are. What I don't understand is why you insist on playing this game with me. You did this last night. Now, again!"

He lowered himself onto the corner of his desk and crossed his arms over his chest, stretching the material of his shirt taut. His slacks tightened over powerful thighs, hard muscles filling them out. The pose was distracting. It flung her into the past until his voice brought her back to the present.

"Suppose you tell me who you think I am."

"Arthur, from maintenance."

"I know who you're referring to, but I'm not him."

"Yes, you are! We sheltered in your cabin, only you had a full dark beard, then."

"Arthur does have a beard. It's gray. So, you must have spent time with someone else. I am curious to know why you think it was me though."

Riley's fingertips pressed against her temples. "We spent a few days together after you rescued me during a snowstorm. You loaned me your clothes after mine got soaked. We built a snowman and made . . ." she stopped before she could remind him how he'd taken her to bed.

"Is that so? That sounds intriguing. When did this happen?"

"A few months ago. Are you suffering from amnesia or something?" Riley asked, knowing she might be risking losing her job by continuing to challenge him.

"I was about to ask you the same thing."

He stood up.

"You obviously believe what you're saying, and I'm sorry if I'm disappointing you, but my name really is Erik King. You may not be aware of it, but Arthur left this site months ago. We needed him elsewhere."

"I know he left. I thought he was you." She touched her head. "You must think I'm crazy."

"A little muddled, perhaps. If you were rescued from a snowstorm as you say, then that traumatic experience could have caused you to be confused. You appear to have a headache right now. The coffee could help. Why don't you let me fix you a cup? How do you take it?"

Riley wanted to shout that he knew very well how she liked her coffee, since he served her so many times at the cabin, but of course she couldn't bring the subject up again. What was the use? He would deny it over and over. An experience so important to her obviously meant nothing to him.

She walked to the counter.

"I'll do the coffee. Should I pour you a cup?"

"No thank you. Come and sit down when you're ready. I'd like to go over a few things, since we will be working together," he explained and went to sit behind the desk.

The big furniture suited his size much better than his sister, considering her grandfather had the desk built for his own tall frame. Riley carried her coffee and sat in one of the chairs, trying to ignore the effect this man seemed to have on her.

"I had hoped you would stay and talk to me a bit more at the party to help make this meeting go easier for you, but I understand your priority was your boyfriend."

"Harve isn't my boyfriend. We've only had a few dates. We were both invited. Just made sense that we would go together."

"I must be getting old. A few dates usually meant you were boyfriend and girlfriend when I was at that phase in my life."

"According to what your sister said last night, you've had plenty of girlfriends."

"My sister thinks she knows everything there is to know about my personal life. She doesn't. Let's talk about you. I've observed a few things, but I'd like to learn more."

He leaned forward and folded his hands on the surface of the desk, drawing Riley's attention. Heat rose in her body as she remembered how good those strong fingers felt when they stroked her naked body. She took a sip of coffee, desperate to compose herself. She might end up making an even bigger fool of herself if these erotic flashbacks didn't stop soon.

"What do you think you know about me?"

"I think you are shy, but not unfriendly. Curious, but not intrusive. You don't care for alcohol and you looked quite lovely in your yellow gown."

"Thank you for the dress compliment," Riley shifted uneasily in her chair, "but I'm not sure if you should be saying such a thing to me."

"It was an observation, not a come on. You needn't worry that our relationship will be anything but business between us. It's important that you understand that upfront. I came here to work, not chase you around my desk."

Riley knew she had every reason to worry, but that was her problem. "Where did Mrs. Blair and her family go, if you don't mind me asking?"

"A cruise to Mexico."

"Really? No offense, but I can't picture Mr. Blair wanting to do something like that."

"Fran's idea, but it will do him good. He tends to take himself too seriously."

"When will she be returning to the office?"

"She doesn't have any plans to return at this point in time."

Another bombshell. She almost choked on her coffee.

"You mean never?" she asked, annoyed that her voice sounded like a squeak. "Why not?"

"She needs more time with her family. I'm taking over here. I've been working at the other sites already. The separate parts need to become more of a whole entity again. I want this company to be up to the quality it once was, and I intend to make that happen."

"Your sister worked hard to keep things running smoothly. I think you owe her that."

"I wasn't being critical. She did the best she could, but the company still hasn't been operating at maximum efficiency. Someone needed to spend time at the other sites. Unfortunately, it was too difficult for Frances to do the necessary travel."

"Well, she does have kids. I'm sure she just wanted to be home as much as possible."

"Now she can be. Things are starting to shape up the way I want at the other sites."

"And you intend to shape up things here to your satisfaction, is that it?"

"That is correct. However, I won't be able to be here every day. That's why it's imperative that I have someone to take care of things when I'm away at the other offices. I've been working with the assistants at the various sites long enough to be confident they are doing well and understand what I expect from them."

"Now you want to train me, so I can handle the work like they do. Just tell me what you want me to do and I'll do it."

"In a moment. You should know I suggested putting one of the other ladies in charge here because they all have more experience than you do. I wanted you to hear that directly from me and not from office gossip. My sister believes you can handle whatever responsibilities I give you. However, I prefer to be my own judge. It won't take me long to see if she's right about you. I'm not a patient man. Don't expect me to carry you if you can't keep up."

Riley's coffee cup made a slight bang on the desk, as she surged to her feet.

"You needn't worry about me not being able to keep up. I was raised with a strong work ethic. That plus everything Frances taught me should satisfy your exacting principles."

"We'll see."

"Is there anything else you wanted to say to me, Mr. King?"

"Yes. I sent a list of things to your desk that I want you to get started on." He glanced down at his watch. "I have a couple of conference calls to make. I'll expect you to be ready to show me what progress you've made as soon as I'm done. That will be your first test. Think you can handle it?"

"I can handle a lot of things, sir," she said with heavy emphasis on the sir before she stomped out of the room, barely stopping herself from slamming the door.

Erik watched her go. He didn't know what was going to happen between them, but he had a feeling the days ahead were probably going to prove quite interesting, considering Riley's obvious spirit. Either they would learn to work together in some form of harmony or end up squaring off like a couple of combatants heading into battle.

He found himself looking forward to the challenges.

It didn't take Riley long to discover he was an unrelenting taskmaster. The mantle of authority suited him well. He was a tyrant to work for. She supposed he'd have to be considering the grueling work schedule he kept for himself. He piloted the company plane back and forth between the offices. His efforts were starting to pay off, as ELK gradually began to climb back up to its previous status. Riley worked as hard as she ever had doing her job, determined not to fail.

She often wished Erik gone when he was there and missed him when he was away. The man really was going to drive her crazy. She still couldn't shake the idea that he was the one who rescued her and made love to her in that remote cabin. Yet, although they worked closely together and she spent literally hours alone with him, he never gave any indication he enjoyed being near her.

Time to accept that she was just another worker in ELK's now well-oiled machine. Her only use to him was how well she did her job. She hadn't forgotten how he practically told her so, in the beginning when he thought she wouldn't be able to keep up with the workload. She was determined to prove him wrong. Her stubbornness refused to let him be right; her pride demanded it.

Riley didn't have much time for a social life these days. Harve had given up on her; he now had *a* real girlfriend. During the few times when Frances came to the office. Riley never let her know what a strain it was to work for her brother. Frances' confidence in her made Riley strive not to let her down.

Another week ended, and Riley had accepted an invitation to join a couple of ladies from work for dinner out. She did this every now and then, so they wouldn't think she was a total snob. But she was home in her apartment now, and all she wanted to do was prop her feet on the coffee table, sit back, and check her cell for messages. She dug into her purse seconds before she remembered tossing the phone into her top desk drawer when Erik walked out of his office.

Having him catch her using her personal phone during work hours wouldn't exactly earn her any extra kudos. Well, no way was she going to go phoneless all weekend. She scooted off the couch and shrugged into her jacket. A quick trip to the office wouldn't take long. She had a key, after all, and knew the alarm security code. In. Out. She'd have her phone. No problem.

Riley stood frowning at the key in her hand. The outer office door was unlocked. Erik always locked up on the days he was here. The man may have a lot on his mind, but he wouldn't forget something so important. His office door stood ajar with a narrow strip of light spilling out.

Riley glanced at her watch. Ten o'clock at night and he was still working. Didn't he ever go home? She jammed her cell into a pocket, ready to leave. She'd rather he didn't know she was here because he might think forgetting her phone signified carelessness. The exit was mere steps away when she stopped. What if he became ill and was too incapacitated to call for help?

She shook her head. The man was too arrogant to be sick. But he could have fallen and possibly hit his head. He might be lying on the floor right now, bleeding. She made a face at such a wild idea, took a couple of steps, and stopped again. He hated to be interrupted while he was working, but he couldn't chastise her for showing concern. What to do?

Conscience blotted out imagination.

She pushed his door open, soundless on well-oiled hinges. The desk lamp cast a wide beam of light across Erik's face. Riley inched her way forward on footsteps muted by thick carpeting.

"Erik?" He raised his head, his expression so bleak it reminded her of a wounded animal . . . not the strong, invincible man she'd come to know. It was like a stab to her heart seeing his obvious pain and not wondering about the cause. What could have created such a transformation?

She had to know.

Chapter Six

Everything about Erik suggested a man beaten down. Slumped shoulders. Hands pressed to either side of his head. Eyes dull. Deep lines creasing his forehead and furrowing his cheeks.

She was on shaky ground and she knew it, but Riley couldn't stop herself.

"I don't care what you say your name is or who you are, I'm in love with you."

"Riley," he choked out in a hoarse voice and shifted in his chair.

"I need you, and I'm pretty darn sure you need me. Please don't send me away."

"Riley," he said again, and this time her name sounded almost like a prayer.

She walked to his desk, moved in, cupped his face between her hands, and covered his lips with her mouth wanting to do anything she could to erase his tortured expression. A deep shudder went through him while emotions threatened to consume them both. She forced herself to pull away after several seconds, shaken by the intensity of her feelings.

"I need to know something before this goes any further. No more games. Only the truth. I realize I probably rushed you at the cabin into trying to establish a bond between us that you weren't ready for. But you are the man who made love to me, aren't you?"

He tugged her onto his lap and wrapped his arms around her waist.

"Yes, and not a day goes by that I don't think of how good it felt to hold you."

"Then why did you pretend otherwise? I've been going out of my mind trying to understand why you were denying we'd never met before your grandfather's party. How could you be so cruel when you knew I was in love with you the day we left the cabin?"

"Correction. You were in love with a man named Arthur. I wanted to bring you closer by having you love the real me."

"You may have wanted to bring me closer, but you were pushing me away by the way you've been treating me. You confused me so much I didn't know what to think. Do you know how hard it is to love someone and not have them love you back? I've worked by your side for months, and you barely noticed me except for what I could do for you in the job."

"You're wrong. I noticed everything about you. The scent of your perfume. The softness of your hair when it brushed against me. The touch of your fingers when you handed me anything. The sound of your voice long after I left the office. I have shared in your pain, believe me."

"This may sound selfish, but it's nice to know I haven't been the only one hurting."

"You hid it well, Riley."

She gave his shoulder a light punch.

"Look who's talking. You totally concealed your emotions, reducing me to nothing more than just another office-girl. And oh, I longed for so much more."

"It wasn't easy. I love you, Riley. I needed you, but you've mostly just shown me anger. I assume that was because of the quantity and quality of work I demanded. Have I lost you?"

"No. Although, you did throw down the gauntlet that first day, and I had to prove to you I was equal to your challenge. I do love you, but you really are a tyrant to work for, Erik."

"I couldn't play favorites. I had to drive everyone equally, but you especially being my assistant if I was going to be able to turn this company around. Being considered a tyrant is the least of what people think I am. They just do a better job of hiding their feelings now."

"Did you keep your identity a secret at the cabin because you were worried what I'd think?"

"Yes. People here gossip. I couldn't take the chance you may believe what you heard. You were going to be stuck inside with me. I was afraid you would panic if you knew my real name."

"All I ever heard was you worked in the field-testing new equipment. I thought you were selfish not to be here for Frances more, but that's all."

"No, that isn't all. People around here think I'm responsible for a woman's death. Some have even gone so far as to say I'm a murderer. Oh, not to my face, but I've heard the whispers."

"A murderer!" Stunned, Riley reared back and searched his face. "You can't be serious."

"Do you think I would joke about something like that?"

"No, but to call you a murderer is pretty drastic. Why would anyone even say such a thing?"

Erik jabbed his thumb to an 8 x 10 glossy photo on his desk.

"Because of this."

A picture of men, women, and a couple children standing by a large inflatable raft drew Riley's attention. Everyone was smiling, including Erik. She didn't understand what this had to do with people calling him a

50

murderer. But whatever the reason she had a feeling it was a vital clue to why he had shut himself away and why he looked so miserable when she came in here.

"I know ELK sometimes offers rafting tours. Did something happen after this was taken?"

He pointed to one of the women.

"She died. And it was my fault."

Riley closed her eyes for a moment, recalling how she teased him about hiding in his cabin because of a woman breaking his heart. This must be the woman. She realized now he hadn't been suffering from a broken heart as much as grief over this person's death.

She opened her eyes.

"I'm so sorry, Erik. Will you tell me how it was your fault?"

"She fell overboard while I was steering the raft and lost control. I jumped into the water thinking to save her, but I almost ended up drowning myself."

"Oh my God. What about the others? What did they do?"

"The woman's husband went in after her, but he was too late by the time he reached her. Another man dove in to grab me. I'm usually a strong swimmer, but my body felt like lead. If I didn't know better, I would have sworn weights were tied to my arms and legs."

"I thought people were supposed to wear some kind of lifejacket on those rafting trips."

"We all did, but mine came undone."

"Isn't that odd, considering your experience wearing them? Why did yours come undone?"

"I hadn't secured it properly."

"Let me back up here for a minute and recap. You lost control of the raft; you didn't do up your lifejacket properly; and you almost drowned because your body felt like lead. It sounds like you were ill. I'm surprised you didn't ask someone else in the company to take your place."

"I wasn't ill. I was drugged," he said, jaw going tense. "It just didn't hit me right away."

"Drugged! You? I don't believe it."

"Riley, I tested positive. Richard Melvin, the man who lost his wife told the authorities he thought I was acting strange right after we started the trip. He demanded I be tested. I didn't try to fight him on it because I wanted to know myself why I screwed up so badly."

"Okay, but I know you're not an addict, so how could drugs have gotten into your system?"

"I don't know. The only thing I put in my body was coffee, from the thermos Wayne brought from Frances. My sister certainly wouldn't drug me."

"Did anyone check the thermos?"

Erik shook his head.

"No. I left it with Wayne, but he said he accidentally dropped it in the water right after the trip started. The thermos was never found."

"Did anyone else drink from the thermos? Wayne, maybe?"

"No. He was supposed to go with me on the trip, but he woke up feeling sick that morning. He did do what he could by bringing the thermos and helping me get everything ready."

Riley pointed to a muscular man in the photo.

"Is that Mr. Melvin sitting by his wife?"

"Yes. He broke down and sobbed over her body. I tried to apologize, but he didn't want to hear it. Who could blame him? He sent me a picture of his wife in her coffin at her funeral." Erik's hands fisted on the arms of his chair. "Not exactly an image easy to get out of my head."

Riley rubbed his arm in soothing strokes. "That's so unfair. You did try to save her."

"And failed. But at least Melvin didn't come out of it totally empty handed."

"What do you mean?"

"He sued ELK and came away with enough money to make him a wealthy man."

"You shut yourself away because of guilt, and I made fun of you. I'm so sorry."

Erik shrugged away her apology.

"You didn't know the circumstances, and I certainly couldn't tell you. I did try to go back to work right after the accident, but I couldn't seem to focus on anything but the accident. I wasn't any good to anyone, including myself."

"You were good for me. I wouldn't be here if you hadn't rescued me in that snowstorm."

"Actually, you're the one who saved me. You made me want to live my life again. I wanted to be with you, but I knew that wasn't going to happen unless I came back to my life here."

Her eyes softened with love. "I made you want to live again, really? That's probably the nicest compliment anyone has ever given me. You know I love you and I want us to be together, but I think you are still carrying around too much guilt from the rafting accident. I also think you won't ever be fully free of those feelings unless you find out what really happened."

Erik rapped his knuckles on top of the photo.

"I just told you what happened."

"Yes, but you don't know why. Someone must have drugged your coffee. Why? I bet that same someone tampered with your lifejacket. Again, why? Who benefited from this tragedy?"

"That would be Richard Melvin if you consider money was more important to him than losing his wife. But I don't believe that. I told you he cried."

"Most people can whip up a few tears if they have to." Riley put her finger to Erik's lips when he started to protest. "I'm not saying this man wanted his wife dead, but a lot of people do bad things if enough money is involved. He had to know a successful company like ELK would have the funds to pay if they were sued. Did anyone actually see his wife fall overboard?"

"Only him."

"Mr. Melvin looks like a strong guy, and his petite wife sat right next to him. It would be pretty easy for him to give her a little shove when everyone else's attention was elsewhere."

Erik's eyes widened in surprise. "Jesus, Riley, that's a hell of a thing to say. Who in their right mind would do such a thing? But even if you are right, that doesn't explain how he drugged my coffee and tampered with my lifejacket without anyone seeing him."

"Did you personally check all the lifejackets before everyone got into the raft?"

"Wayne took care of those and please don't tell me you think he had anything to do with what happened. That would be as ridiculous as saying Fran drugged my coffee."

No missing the hint of warning in his tone. Time to steer away from talking about Wayne Blair.

"Oh no, of course not. But getting back to Mr. Melvin, how much do you know about him? Like what did he do for a living before he got all that money in the lawsuit? What did he buy once he became rich? Were he and his wife happily married?"

"I don't know any of that, and I didn't want to know. What does it matter? Geraldine Melvin died, and nothing will bring her back. I just hope the money helped him to move on with his life. The authorities ruled it an accident. I'm lucky I didn't end up in jail."

Riley could have said he created his own jail when he shut himself away in his cabin. But he'd suffered enough already. She would much rather try to help him break free of his guilt.

"I went to school with a girl who really was quite attractive, but her mother told her she was homely. I think the woman was jealous of her own daughter. Anyway, the girl might have saved herself a lot of heartache if she believed the evidence of what she saw in her mirror. But she thought because it was her mom who said she was homely then it must be true."

"What does that story have to do with my situation?"

"The point I'm trying to make is authorities aren't always right. You believed them because they're supposed to be the experts. How thorough was the investigation? It seems like the questions I just asked you would have come up at the time all the details were being gathered."

"My grandfather wanted to get everything over with as quickly as possible. The accident brought quite a bit of bad publicity to the company. We said what we had to say and paid the money to the grieving widower. Now if you don't mind, I'd rather not talk about it anymore. I should never have brought it up in the first place. This is a hell of a way to have our reunion."

"You're right. I didn't mean to upset you." She touched a fingertip to the gray shadows smudged beneath his eyes. "You look tired. Have you been getting much sleep?"

"Not much."

"You've been working too hard."

"It was the only way I could stop thinking about how much I wanted to be with you."

"Then come home with me right now."

"I . . ." His cell phone rang at that moment making him lean over toward his desk and check the screen. "Give me a minute," he sighed and answered. The conversation was brief with Erik's replies abrupt to the point of bordering on rudeness.

"You don't seem very happy. Is everything okay?" Riley asked as soon as he ended the call.

"That was my grandfather asking when I'd be home."

"I heard you say you would be staying elsewhere tonight. Did he want to know where?"

"No, but he mentioned condoms." Erik snorted in disgust. "I've got to get my own place!"

Riley put a hand over her mouth to stifle a giggle at his indignant expression. "I have a very comfortable bed large enough for two and plenty of closet space in my apartment if you're interested in moving in with me."

"I'm very interested. But there's something I'd like to make clear before we do. I don't want to cheapen our relationship by sneaking around. I would rather people know we're a couple, especially at work. Is that going to be a problem after what I told you about their reaction to the accident?"

"I don't care what the gossips will say. I'd shout it from the top of a mountain that I want us to be together if I could." Riley scooted off his lap. "I'll wait while you lock up, so you can follow me and see where I live."

"I already know where you live."

"You do? That's a surprise."

"I doubt that. No more games, remember? You honestly don't think I wouldn't have driven by your place on the days I work here."

The very idea that he'd been thinking about her as much as she'd been pining for him made Riley mentally forgive him for the several months of unhappiness she had suffered.

They walked into her apartment together. Erik locked the door. He stood with his back to Riley. The sound of him expelling a long-ragged breath worried her he was already regretting saying he wanted them to be a couple. She told him she didn't care what people said, but maybe the added pressure would end up being one more hurdle for him to clear. The main thing was not to drive him away like she did the day they left the cabin.

"Erik, it's okay if you want to take more time to think about this. I understand the ramifications of us being together now that you've told me about the accident. We can wait."

He took her in his arms.

"I've wasted enough time. I'm ready to give you tomorrow now."

Whatever feelings Riley experienced when Erik made love to her before only heightened what he made her feel tonight. Exciting. Explosive. Arousing. Incredibly intoxicating. They enjoyed each other long into the night as time became less about sex and more about making love. Her dream about waking up next to this man every day for the rest of her life was now going to become a reality.

But when she opened her eyes in the morning and stretched out her hand, she encountered empty space where she expected to touch Erik's warm body. Riley sprang up rubbing the sleep out of her eyes. She called his name. No answer. She scrambled out of bed and padded barefoot over to the double windows overlooking the parking area searching for any sign of his car.

No car. No Erik. Why did he leave after he promised to stay? Riley stood in the living room fighting the bitter swell of disillusionment invading her chest. Seconds elapsed before she began to inhale the unmistakable aroma of coffee drifting through the air urging her into action. One bare foot came close to smacking into an end table in her haste to reach the kitchen. Her eyes went straight to the coffee maker with its freshly brewed pot. A mug sat on the counter . . . and a note. She grabbed the paper with a sense of trepidation.

The information would either make her day, or seriously mess up her life. She took a moment to admire his bold handwriting before devouring every bit of information. Erik received a message from the Anchorage site that required his immediate attention. He hoped to return tomorrow and asked that she clear a space in her closet for his clothes. He closed by thanking her for an amazing night. She pressed her lips to his name and vow of love.

"He does want you, but he still has to work, dummy," she scolded to the empty room.

She poured a cup of coffee and carried it to the bathroom. She showered and dressed in sweats, soft and comfortable from numerous washings. Erik's absence would give her a chance to research Richard Melvin. Riley couldn't explain why, but looking at him in the photo set off a signal strong enough to make her itch to know more about the man.

Her dad always said if you have an itch, you should scratch it.

A couple hours later Riley sat back and went over the data she collected. No wonder she had such bad vibes about the man. The unfortunate woman who died in the river was the fourth Mrs. Melvin. Wife number one fell off a cliff while vacationing with her husband. Wifey number two succumbed to a venomous snakebite, also while vacationing with hubby dearest. The third Mrs. Melvin choked to death on a piece of food while having a private candlelight dinner with Mr. Melvin in their hotel suite.

Four very unlucky ladies.

No surprise to read he was the one who hauled in hefty amounts of money from all the ladies' insurance policies. It would seem going on vacation with Richard Melvin always turned out to be a one-way ticket for his women. Riley thought about doing more searching when her phone pinged an incoming call. She hoped to see Erik's name show up, but it was her friend Tanny from Hawaii. That made her smile. She loved talking with Tanny.

"Hey there, how are things?" Riley asked in a cheerful voice.

"Couldn't be better. We are now officially honorary aunties."

Riley scooted her chair back and jumped up. "Did Tessa have her baby?"

"She sure did, a little over an hour ago. Ian junior has arrived, weighing in at a whopping eight pounds, five ounces, and with a full head of dark hair like his daddy."

"I bet Ian is absolutely beyond happy and Rea must be thrilled to have a new baby brother."

"He can't stop smiling and Rea thinks the baby is her very own living doll. Tessa wanted me to call you right away and give you the good news."

"I'm so glad you did. How is Tessa doing?"

"Great. She'll talk to you when things have a chance to settle down a bit."

"I look forward to it. How about you? I know your baby girl is due pretty soon."

"Not soon enough. I'm waddling around in my muumuu looking more like an over inflated cow. Caleb says I look beautiful. I told him he must need glasses."

Riley laughed.

"Love is supposed to make you blind, but I bet you do look fabulous."

"More like fatulous."

Riley laughed again. "How is it every time we talk, you make me feel so lighthearted?"

"I don't know, but I'm glad. Tessa and I thought you sounded a little down in our last few phone calls. We were thinking you may be homesick or maybe had man trouble."

"A little of both at the time, but I'm feeling a whole lot better now."

"My female radar tells me a man is part of why you feel better. What's he like?"

"I'll talk about him later. It's too new now, but I can tell you he makes great coffee."

"Well then, he's a keeper."

Minutes later Riley's phone rang again, but this time the call did not bring good news.

Frances was calling with the news that Erik's plane had crashed. Riley's body went weak. Sickness surged into her throat. Trembling fingers were barely able to hold onto her phone.

"Is he . . ." Where were the words when you needed them?

"He survived," Frances cut in. "But he does have injuries."

"Will you please keep me updated? He, um, is my boss after all."

"I know he's more than that to you, Riley. That's why I'm calling. It would be a good idea if you came to the hospital right away."

"Yes, all right."

People still died after a plane crash . . . even if they initially survived.

Please, God.

There were no words.

Chapter Seven

Riley thanked Frances and dashed out the door grabbing her purse on the run. It didn't matter that she wasn't wearing any makeup, her sweats looked shabby, and her hair flopped around her face in disarray. All she cared about was getting to Erik as quickly as possible.

Every red light made her gnash her teeth, and it didn't help being stalled by what seemed like the slowest drivers on the planet. She arrived at the hospital fuming with impatience, scrambled out of the car, ran to the front entrance, and yanked open the door. She burst into the building in a flurry of movement, dodged a couple wheelchair patients, and a gurney before she reached a station to ask the location of the all-important room number.

She had her directions now and continued to rush forward, her tennis shoes making little squeaky sounds on the smooth floor. Riley rounded a corner and stopped when she saw Ernest, Wayne, and Edward. She was hoping for Frances. The men had spaced themselves apart from each other without a hint of camaraderie among them. Wayne stood leaning against a wall staring at the floor with his hands in his pockets. Edward's fingers moved busily over the surface of his phone, while Ernest paced the hallway.

Riley approached Wayne being the closest and the only one she really knew.

He looked up.

"Frances said she called you." He pointed to Edward. "That's Erik's father. You may have seen him in the office."

Riley managed a mere quirking of her lips forming a thin smile. Edward sent her a silent, petulant look before returning his attention back to his phone. Wayne introduced her to Ernest next. His reaction was more vocal and laced with unabashed cynicism.

"So, this is the wench my grandson's been going on about? Kind of on the skinny side."

"For heaven's sake, Ernest!" Wayne protested.

Enough people around the office had described Ernest King as being a very critical person. Riley wished their first meeting could have been under less stressful circumstances and with the support of Erik or Frances to bolster her confidence. But she reminded herself she was here to see Erik, not to impress his grandfather. Still, the urge to finger comb her hair and wished she'd worn makeup did cross her mind for a moment until she steeled herself not to be intimidated by the old bully.

"I guess I am slender, but that's probably because I'm from Hawaii and I grew up eating coconuts and pineapples, instead of whale blubber."

Ernest's bushy eyebrows rose for a moment and then he chuckled. "You've got spunk, girl."

Frances came out of Erik's room at that moment and hurried to Riley. "Everything okay?"

"I hope so," she replied, sneaking a wary look at Ernest from beneath her lashes.

Frances pulled her away from the men. "Erik's been asking for you."

"Thank God. I wasn't sure if he would be conscious. How badly is he hurt?"

"Gash on the head needing stitches, cracked ribs, and a nasty sprained ankle."

"Ouch! Makes me wince just thinking about the pain he must be suffering."

"More than he should be, but he's refusing to take any medication."

"That doesn't sound very smart. Is it because he's being macho?"

"No, it's because . . . never mind. Go see him. I'm going to go talk to a nurse."

Small wonder he didn't want to take medication now considering he was drugged the day of the river accident. But this was a whole different situation and the drugs would be carefully monitored. She may mention that. She eased the door open just enough to peer into the room.

A large bruise like a splash of purple dye highlighted the puffiness on one side of his face. The white dressing covering his stitches made a striking contrast against his skin. Flesh surrounding his swollen ankle stretched taut where his foot created an indention on a large pillow. His lips twisted into a grimace and she heard the unmistakable sound of a quick, sharp intake of breath, as he shifted his body on the bed.

Riley knew she would have inquired about his pain medication herself if Frances hadn't already explained the situation. She pushed the door all the way open announcing her presence.

"Knock, knock."

"And look who's here. Thanks for coming."

"As if I wouldn't." She walked over to his bed, relieved to see him so alert. "I know you said you wanted to leave your grandfather's house, but isn't this a bit drastic?"

Riley thought he would appreciate humor more than her showing just how upset she was really feeling. She leaned over and gave him a soft kiss on the cheek.

"I think we can do better than that."

He put one hand behind her head, another on her shoulder, and drew her close enough to cover her lips with his mouth. A fine film of sweat dampened his brow after a few seconds and his fingers gripped her with more pressure than pleasure. Riley eased herself back away.

"You're hurting and don't try to deny it. I can see it in your face."

"A face that looks like I used it as a battering ram. I'm not complaining considering I could be a lot worse. I'm sorry about leaving you so abruptly, but I didn't have the heart to wake you."

"I might have talked you into staying if you did. Thanks for the coffee and note."

"I guess you realize now I'll have to wait until I recover before I can move in with you."

"Tanny took care of Caleb after he was hurt. Why don't you let me take care of you?"

He shook his head just enough to cause him to wince. "Thanks for the offer, but I don't want to begin our domesticity as an invalid. I did mention our plans about cohabiting to Fran."

"Does she approve?"

"Riley, I do not need permission from my sister to choose where I live. But she thinks my injuries are serious enough to need a nurse when I leave here, which can't be too soon for me."

"For goodness sake, you just survived a plane crash. You need to give your body a chance to heal. Please don't try to rush things. Oh, and take the pain medication the doctor ordered."

"What makes you think I'm not?"

"Don't try to weasel your way out of giving me a straight answer. I don't think, I know you aren't t taking your pills. But Frances is getting your meds as we speak."

He sighed

"I should have known."

"She's your family. You know very well she only wants what's best for you. Too much pain can inhibit healing. And speaking of family, I just met your grandfather."

"I thought he would have gone home by now. I'm almost afraid to ask what he said to you."

"He thinks I'm skinny."

Erik rolled his eyes toward the ceiling.

"First time you meet, and he dishes out insults. Welcome to my world." He squeezed her hand. "Don't take it personally. He's a rude old man."

"I heard that about him, so I wasn't going to let him bully me. I told him I'm slender because I grew up eating coconuts and pineapples, instead of whale blubber."

A flicker of amusement brightened Erik's painfilled eyes for a moment.

"What a great comeback. I wish I could have seen the expression on his face. What did he say, or did you leave him speechless?"

"He said I had spunk. I think my comment surprised him."

"You probably did. Good for you. He needs to be surprised now and then."

"I saw your father in the hallway, too. It's nice he came to see you."

"Don't give him any credit. He came because my grandfather threatened to cut his monthly allowance if he didn't. You could say he's being paid to be here."

Now it was her turn to give his hand a reassuring squeeze. "I'm sorry. That really is sad."

"So is my relationship with him, but I'd rather not talk about that particular subject."

"Can you tell me what sent you to Anchorage, or is it a company secret?"

"Not a secret, but more of a puzzle. Supposedly, some employee fell off a high ladder in the warehouse, hit his head, and died."

A look of confusion crossed Riley's face.

"What do you mean by 'supposedly'?"

"Fran called the warehouse superintendent to tell him about my crash and said she would handle the unfortunate accident in the warehouse while I recovered. He was more concerned about me and told her he had no idea what accident she was referring to."

"Then what the heck was that message you received? Did she tell him about that?"

"Yes. She found out the number belonged to a man working in the warehouse who says someone stole his phone. She believes him. I didn't try to get a hold of anyone else after I got the message because it was so early. I decided I'd do the flight and count it as my usual visit."

Riley stroked the back of his hand. "I'm becoming very frightened for your safety. First you almost drowned, then someone lures you by faking an accident knowing you would fly, and now your plane crashes. What are the odds of that happening to one person?"

"Slim, I suppose. But who knows what really happened on the river that day? And while it's true I was duped into flying, planes do crash. I think I better get myself a good luck charm."

"I'd buy you a dozen if I thought they would help."

Erik ran a fingertip down her cheek. "I'm going to be okay. What did you do after I left?"

"Researched Mr. Melvin. I hope you won't mind, but I just couldn't resist."

"I guess I shouldn't be surprised, knowing the way you questioned me about him." Erik leaned back against the two pillows at his back. "You may as well tell me what you found."

She toyed with his fingers. "I'm sure there was a murderer on the raft, but it wasn't you."

"That's nice to know."

"I'm being serious here."

"So am I. I take it your theory involves what you discovered in your research."

"Yes, it does and with good reason. I believe Richard Melvin went on the rafting trip that day with the sole intention of murdering his wife."

Erik snatched his hand away. "Jesus, Riley. That's a hell of a thing to say."

"Well, murder is a hell of a thing, wouldn't you agree?"

"Yes, but you are talking about a man who lost his wife."

"A wife he wanted to lose," she replied with a stubborn set to her chin.

"What brought you to that drastic conclusion?"

"The man collects wives."

"Riley, people collect stamps, not wives."

"Well, this guy does. Maybe we should talk more about this later. That's what I planned to do. It's not exactly a pleasant topic of conversation for someone who is trying to recover from injuries."

"It wouldn't be pleasant under any circumstances, but you've gone too far to stop now."

"Well, if you're sure."

"Riley," he sighed. "Please just get on with it."

"Okay. The woman on the raft, Geraldine Melvin was his fourth wife. He ended up getting huge amounts of money from their life insurance policies after each wife died in an accident. Strange coincidence they all died accidentally don't you think?"

"Sounds more criminal than accidental, if you're right. I'm surprised you were able to get all that information. How did you manage to find out so much about him?"

"I typed in his name and different profiles came up, but the photos all looked something like Richard Melvin. He didn't change his looks much. Mostly he dyes his hair, changes the style, and sometimes wears some form of facial hair, but he always keeps his body in shape. I also found all his wives' obits online."

"That would mean Melvin set me up, so he could kill his wife and rake in the insurance money. But why risk being exposed when he sued ELK on top of it?"

Riley shrugged.

"Greed, or probably to add more weight to his claim you were at fault."

"So, Melvin enhanced his own life while he destroyed mine. And to think I felt sorry for him!" An obscenity slipped out between Erik's clenched teeth.

"I should have waited until you were feeling better before I told you. But now that I have, I think we should try to find out more."

"What's the point? He got what he wanted, and I had to move on. It's a closed case."

"It's only a closed case as long as you make it be one. Erik, this man killed an innocent woman and tried to destroy you. Let's try to clear your good name and your company's. I may have only scratched the surface on Richard Melvin. My friends in Hawaii are very good at research. I'd like your permission to ask them to see if they can find out anything else that might help your cause. It's not fair that a man like Richard Melvin shouldn't pay for his crimes. Think about the other innocent women he killed."

"This isn't just about me, Riley. I wouldn't want anything to come back to haunt my family. They've already been through enough and Frances still suffers."

"I know. But I would be sure to ask my friends to only report to me if they find out anything that may be significant. I will tell you and then you decide what you'd want to do with the information. You need to have closure, Erik. Even Frances would understand that."

"All right. I trust you and your friends to be discreet."

"We . . ."

Ernest entered the room at that moment making Riley close her mouth.

"I'm leaving now. How long are you staying, girl?"

"Stop calling her girl. Her name is Riley," Erik snapped.

"What kind of a name is that? Did your parents have something against normal names?"

"I don't know what you mean by normal. My mother knew she wasn't going to be able to give me herself, so she gave me her maiden name. She died a few hours after I was born."

Veins swelled where his hand gripped the door handle. "You'll do," he mumbled and left.

Riley cocked her head at Erik. "Did I just receive your grandfather's seal of approval?"

"Small price to pay for his behavior, the old goat. I'm sorry about your mother. It must have been tough growing up without her. Did she have parents who could help your dad with you?"

"They lived on the mainland and rarely visited, but my dad's parents lived on the island and they were great. They're all gone now, too. But I have a lot of good memories about my dad's parents because I spent quite a bit of time in their home while my dad worked. One of my favorite things was watching old movies with them on

TV. Gramps would pop popcorn and we'd share a bowl together. Lots of butter and salt. Terribly unhealthy, but oh so yummy."

"Sounds nice. Funny the things we remember about when we were growing up. You already know there wasn't a lot of affection in my family, but I do recall Frances and I eating breakfast with my grandfather most mornings before we went to school and he left for the office. He always made our toast himself. He would butter it and add marmalade. He acted like he was giving us some great prize. I couldn't stand the stuff, but Fran told me not to say anything."

"I think the bigger prize was having him offer it to you. That may have been his effort to show you affection in the only way he knew how. It also sounds like he really wanted you and Frances to spend that time with him. If he didn't care about you, he wouldn't have asked."

"I never thought of that possibility."

"Those are just some of my thoughts. I could be totally wrong about his reasons."

"No, I think you're probably right. Thanks for pointing it out. I don't know why it's so damn difficult for him to just come out and talk about his feelings."

"Perhaps it's because he never had anyone to show him. Lots of people in the world are like your grandfather. My mom's parents never told me they loved me, and they didn't visit me much. I guess it was too difficult for them because my dad said I looked a lot like my mother."

"Maybe they were afraid of losing you, too, so they wouldn't allow themselves to get too close," Erik said seconds before his eyelids fluttered and slowly closed.

"Now you pointed out something I didn't think about. Go to sleep. I'll check back later."

She kissed him lightly on the lips and tiptoed from the room, her mind already plotting how to relieve Erik from the burden of guilt now that he gave her the go-ahead. She and her friends stopped a monster before who preyed on the innocent.

Time to see if they could do it again.

Chapter Eight

Riley made her call as soon as she arrived back at her apartment.

"Tanny."

"Hey there."

"How are Tessa and the new little one doing?"

"Things are going well from what I hear. Everything still all right with you?"

"I'm fine, but in a bit of a dilemma. I've started something. and I need your help to hopefully finish it. Are you busy now?"

"I'm not busy; and I'd much rather hear about your dilemma than sit here knitting booties."

Riley's brows rose in surprise. "I didn't know you knew how to knit."

"I don't. That's why I'd rather talk to you. What's going on?"

"It's kind of a long story and will take a few minutes to explain."

"I like long stories."

"Okay, here goes."

Riley explained how Erik rescued her in the snowstorm and she fell in love with him after spending several days in his cabin. She went on to say he ended up being her boss and the deception about his identity. Next, she launched into the details about the river tragedy and that now Erik had survived a plane crash. The last thing she revealed was her research on Richard Melvin.

"So, what do you think?"

"I think you should have told us you almost died in a snowstorm. Shame on you, but I'll let that go for now. I'm glad your Erik is going to be all right. This Melvin guy sounds like a real prince. No wonder you think he was up to no good."

"He reminds me of Diesel," she said, mentioning the name of the murderous thug who made life hell for her and her friends before their combined efforts sent him to prison.

"He almost makes Diesel sound like a Boy Scout. So, what can I do to help?"

"I need your expertise in research. I know you did great gathering the information that helped free your dad when he was railroaded into prison. I'd like to get as much info on Richard Melvin that I possibly can. Anything and everything will do. No stone unturned kind of thing."

"I'll get right on it. I'd also like to bring Ian and Caleb in on the search. Ian will be a big help in digging for financial stuff. You said this Melvin lives in Miami, Florida and you thought he looked like he worked out on a regular basis. I'll ask Caleb to look into gyms in the area."

"You've already thought of things I wouldn't have. But I promised Erik you would only report to me. He doesn't want to involve his family, if he can avoid that. He's trusting me to be responsible, and I don't want to blow it."

"I'll tell the guys. One of us will call you as soon as we have anything to report."

"I appreciate this more than you know. Richard Melvin nearly ruined Erik."

"Well then, let's see if we can put a few nicks in the conniving Mr. Melvin's life."

Frances called Riley the next afternoon.

"We just brought Erik home from the hospital."

"Already? I thought the doctor would want to keep him for at least another day."

"He did, but my obstinate brother insisted he wanted out. I thought it best to go along with him before he started tying bedsheets into a chain and lowering himself out a window. He wanted to refuse having a home nurse, but I played on his sympathy and told him I had neither the time nor the expertise to dress his headwound."

"I was going to the hospital on my lunchbreak. Would it be okay if I came by the house?"

"Of course. I'm sure he'll call you as soon as he's settled and ask to see you. Riley, I want you to know Erik told me you asked permission to have your friends research Richard Melvin."

Riley's hand tightened on her phone.

"I didn't think he wanted to tell you. I hope you don't think I was deliberately going behind your back."

"I am willing to accept any help to prove my brother's innocence, but it would be best if you didn't mention it to my grandfather or Wayne. They want to forget what happened to Erik."

"His life would be a lot easier if he could personally forget. I hope you aren't angry that Erik told me about the river accident."

"I've never thought it was an accident. It gives me nightmares every time I think of how he could have died that day, and now the plane crash. My brother isn't a cat with nine lives."

"Good thing, since he's already used up two," Riley muttered.

Erik's eyes traveled around his bedroom. *Better than the hospital with all its restrictions, but still a sickroom,* he thought, considering his injuries. Frances wanted to install him in one of the rooms downstairs, but he preferred to be in his own room. That meant climbing stairs and having to have Ernest and Wayne help him because of his injured ankle. He hated that.

He ignored the bottle of pain pills sitting on the table next to his chair. He agreed to have them here to appease Frances. She expected him to keep taking the medication, but he knew he wouldn't. He couldn't forget how drugs rendered him so helpless on the river that fateful day.

The rafting accident brought his mind to Riley's surprising news about Richard Melvin. Must have been some female intuitive thing that made her suspect he wasn't the grieving widower he portrayed. Weakness from his injuries and fury at Melvin pushed him into giving Riley permission to allow her friends to do more research. Erik just hoped the probing wouldn't end up making things worse for his family.

A knock sounded at the door followed by Riley calling his name. He summoned her into the room.

"You should still be in the hospital, you know," she said, coming to stand by his chair.

"The food is a lot better here."

She pointed to the bottle of pills.

"I hope you are you taking those."

"You are not my mother. I'm getting enough of that from Fran. Do you realize you've been here thirty seconds and you haven't even kissed me yet? How about some TLC?"

Riley leaned down and Erik reached up to slide both his hands into her hair. She sank to her knees giving him easier access to her mouth. They kissed, eyes closed, barely restraining their hunger for each other. She eased back after a few seconds and rose to her feet.

Erik grinned. " Better than any pill, but I could use an extra dose. Why did you stop?"

"You just got out of the hospital. Let's not put you back there the same day."

"It would be worth it, but I can see you're going to be stubborn about this."

Riley pointed a finger to her chest. "I'm stubborn? You're the one who's acting like a recalcitrant child refusing to follow the doctor's orders and giving Frances a hard time about having a nurse come here. I must admit the ambiance is a lot nicer here than the hospital, though."

Riley pulled a chair close to Erik and sat down.

"I wanted you to know I called my friends. They will do what they can to help us."

Erik's hand tightened on the arm of his chair for a moment.

"I told Frances."

"I know. I'm glad you did. I wouldn't feel comfortable doing this without her knowledge."

"Nor would I, which is why I brought her into our confidence."

"But she said we shouldn't confide in your grandfather and your brother-in-law."

"Some things are best done in secrecy. I'll explain things to them if it becomes necessary."

Riley didn't miss the slight twitch in Erik's jaw. Time to change the subject.

"Have you told your grandfather you will be moving in with me when you've recovered?"

"Not yet. He likes to be in control and having me here gives him easier access to what I'm doing with the company. But his nagging does get damn tiresome at times."

"Sometimes nagging is a way of showing love."

"That sounds like something Frances would say. I think you two are ganging up on me."

"In a good way." She stood up.

"I need to get back to the office. My lunchbreak is over."

"I give you permission to stay here longer, as your boss."

"Tempting, but the ladies in the office may feel resentful. And you need your rest."

"I hate being made to feel so damn helpless," Erik grumbled.

"Better helpless than dead." Riley covered her mouth with her hand as soon as the words were out.

"Oh God, I can't believe I said that. I'm sorry, Erik. That sounded so insensitive."

"It's a good reminder for me to be thankful I survived another accident."

So, Erik still referred to the raft incident and his plane crash as accidents. Riley wanted to ignore the persistent voice inside her head suggesting someone wanted him dead. Because if she was right, that person might go after Erik a third time.

And everyone knew three strikes meant you were out.

Every day she didn't hear from her friends filled Riley with growing frustration. Maybe she expected too much, and they couldn't find anything. But that didn't prevent her from checking her phone several times a day hoping for news. She almost ended up dropping the slender instrument when she finally did receive a call from Ian five long days later.

"Ian. How is the little one doing?" she asked, remembering what would be important to him.

"I forgot how something so small can be so loud."

"I bet you wouldn't have it any other way."

"Not in a million years," he answered before changing the subject to what he knew she wanted to hear. "Tanny asked us to help you find what we could on this Richard Melvin."

"Yes. Were you able to discover anything?"

"Quite a bit, actually. I'm sorry it took so long to get back to you, but I wanted to be as thorough as possible before I called."

"I'm just thankful you were all willing to help. I was beginning to doubt myself for asking."

"We wouldn't have found out so much if Caleb didn't have a friend who owed him a favor."

"How does a friend of Caleb's figure in this?"

"This particular friend, Ken happens to live in Miami. He also happened to physically bump into Melvin and found himself holding the man's phone."

Riley's eyes widened.

"You mean he's a pickpocket and he stole Melvin's phone?"

"Not stolen, just borrowed at Caleb's request."

"Because of the favor he owed Caleb, I take it?"

"Yes. Ken keeps in shape and usually works out at home, but he went to Melvin's gym. He had the phone long enough to get some very useful information and send it on to me."

"I appreciate his help, but I hope he didn't get caught."

"Not to worry. He got the phone back before it was even missed. Now, down to business. Melvin has either grown careless or cocky since he's gotten away with his schemes for so long. Either way, he had a lot of data on his phone, including air travel plans."

"Travel plans? Okay. And that is significant because. . .?"

"He makes a lot of trips to the Bahamas. I found enough information to make me suspect he has two offshore accounts there. But I wanted to be sure, so Caleb gave Ken the flight info and asked him to hop over and see where Melvin went after he left the airport."

"Let me guess. Ken saw him go into a bank."

"That would be correct."

"Melvin lives in Miami. Why wouldn't he just use a bank there to do his business?"

"He does, but his secret accounts are probably to hide money he doesn't want to pay taxes on. And by the way, he owns four gyms in Florida. The newest and largest is in Miami. The grand opening was a little over a year ago. Gerry's Gym. Tanny found a newspaper article from that day. Melvin claimed he named the gym after his late wife, Geraldine to honor her memory."

Riley's phone suddenly felt quite heavy in her hand. "Oh my God! Geraldine Melvin was the wife Erik tried to save from drowning."

"Yes, I know. Melvin uses a couple of interesting names."

"Interesting in what way?"

"The first one is Drahcir Nivlem."

"Sounds kind of East Indian."

"That's what I thought until my clever Tessa pointed something out to me. I'll spell out the letters to you. Write them on a piece of paper, Riley."

"Hmm, it looks as foreign as it sounds," she said after jotting down the letters.

"I agree. Now reverse the letters in each name starting from the last to the first."

She did as he suggested and stared in disbelief. "It's Richard Melvin spelled backwards."

"Interesting, as I said. He apparently only uses that account now and then, if the data I found on his phone means anything. The other one gets most of his attention. Caleb brought up the possibility Melvin may be blackmailing someone, and this is where the payments go."

"Do you think that might be true?"

"I wouldn't rule it out, considering the kind of man we're dealing with here."

"You said you found two names. What was the other one?"

Ian paused.

"Riley, you understand when you start probing into peoples' lives there's always the chance you might come across something you wish you hadn't."

"Which means I won't want to hear what you're about to say, but I should know."

"The name is Frances Paige."

"I'm not comfortable with the Frances part, but at least the last name isn't Blair. You had me worried there for a . . ."

"Paige happens to be her mother's maiden name," Ian interrupted.

A cold little shiver slid down her spine. "That . . . that could be a coincidence, right?"

"It could be, but you have to admit it's a little too close to home not to wonder."

"But why would Richard Melvin be blackmailing Frances, if that's what is happening?"

"I have no idea. The only way you would be able to find out is to ask her or Melvin, and I seriously doubt if either one of them would be willing to give you a straight answer."

"Right. Thank you for your help. You've given me a lot to think about."

"Let me know if there's anything else we can do from this end."

She cut the connection. What hold could Richard Melvin have on Frances if this was a blackmail situation? She didn't want to point a finger at Frances, but the only way to solve the mystery would be to get it out in the open. The Paige name was too close to Frances. Riley didn't want to just wonder about that . . . she wanted to know. The decision to have Wayne and Erik be included in a meeting would be up to Frances.

If looks were daggers, Riley knew she would be dead, considering the way Wayne continued to glare at her. Her hands gripped the chair arms, as she braced herself for more verbal abuse.

"You have a lot of gall coming here and accusing my wife of being mixed up with someone like Richard Melvin. Is this how you repay her for giving you a job you didn't even deserve?"

"I'm not accusing her. I wanted to help you find out what happened that day on the river."

"What are you talking about? We already know what happened. The authorities did their investigation and closed the case. Are you saying you're better than the law?"

"No, but they obviously didn't investigate everything about Richard Melvin. I thought you would all want to know what my friends discovered during their research."

"That's another thing that burns me. What makes you think you have the right to go asking people we don't even know to start nosing around into our private lives?"

She sent Erik and Frances pleading looks. Both continued to remain silent.

"I looked up Richard Melvin myself and found out some troubling information that worried me enough to ask my friends if they could find out more. That's how the name Frances Paige came up."

"Did you ever stop to think there are probably hundreds of people with the same name?"

"I know, but several of them had photos of him."

"You've never even met the man. How do you know it was him in those pictures?"

Riley sent another helpless look toward Erik. "Well, I . . ."

Wayne continued his ranting. "It's bad enough you hacked into our personal files, but did you ever stop to consider how Melvin might decide to come after my wife if he finds out an employee of ELK is invading his privacy?"

"My friends and I were very discreet. I'm the one who found out about all the marriages. Doesn't it bother you that Richard Melvin had four wives and they all died, so he could end up collecting insurance money?"

"A lot of people have multiple marriages. People die and survivors collect insurance. There isn't anything unusual about that."

"What about the money he got by suing ELK?"

Wayne sliced his hand through the air. "Now you're snooping into the company's affairs. Is there any end to how far you will intrude? I don't care how many wives Richard Melvin had or how much money he got from their insurance policies. That has nothing to do with us. You and your friends should be sued for defamation of character. Not only that, I recommend you be fired for coming here trying to upset the family with your outrageous lies."

"They aren't outrageous. My friend Ian Hawk sent data from Richard Melvin's phone."

"I don't give a damn what he sent you. You're all a bunch of liars and I'll see you in court."

"No one is going to court and Riley won't be fired," Erik finally spoke at last.

"Of course not. You wouldn't want to lose the convenience of having your whore handy."

Frances gasped. "Wayne! That's a terrible thing to say. Apologize to Riley."

"I will do no such thing."

Erik sent Wayne his own frosty glare.

"The only reason you aren't chewing on some broken teeth from me smashing my fist in your face is because I understand you are defending your wife. But if I ever hear you talk about Riley that way again, I promise you will have more than a few missing teeth to worry about."

"Oh, sure, beat up on me because you believe she has all the answers."

"I don't think she has all the answers, but you seem to be arrogant enough to think you do."

Riley shot to her feet.

"Please stop! I never wanted to have family turn against family. I worried Erik's plane crash and him almost drowning in the river may be attempts on his life. That's the reason I wanted to find out more about what happened."

"Attempts on his life. Oh, please!" Wayne snorted. "What a stupid idea."

"Perhaps you wouldn't think it was so stupid if you were the who came close to dying."

"Look, Erik, I don't want you to think I wasn't concerned when you had these accidents, but that's what they were . . . accidents. Riley is trying to stir up trouble.

For God's sake, can't you see she's poisoning your mind with all this garbage she and her friends have concocted?"

Frances touched Wayne on the arm, but he jerked away.

"Please don't be so upset."

"Don't be upset? Is that all you can say? This whole mess started because a woman you trusted decided to take it upon herself to have strangers dig up a name to try and frame you."

"Riley didn't take it upon herself. I gave her my permission to ask her friends to see what they could find out about Richard Melvin."

A small vein began to throb in Wayne's forehead.

"You gave her your permission without telling me?"

He turned and stared at Erik.

"Did you know anything about such an arrangement?"

"Yes. I also told her it would be all right."

"Oh, did you? Well, that's just great! You two made an important family decision without consulting me. I thought I was a member of this family as well, but I guess I was wrong."

"Oh Wayne, of course you're family." Frances reached for his hand, but he yanked it away.

"It's a little late to be trying to pacify me."

He lurched out of his chair, sending it wobbling. "I'll leave you with your coconspirators," he snapped and stormed out of the room.

"Wait, please!" Frances called, but he didn't turn back. "I need to go to him." She gave the others a helpless look seconds before rushing after her husband.

Riley watched her go.

"I think I'd better go now, too. I'm very sorry about all this, Erik."

"I know you just wanted to help. Don't worry, I'm sure Frances will calm him down."

"I think we both know he isn't going to calm down until either we prove or disapprove whether or not the name Frances Paige had anything to do with your family. That is, if you still want to keep going with this."

Erik rubbed a hand around the back of his neck. "Truthfully? I'm not sure anymore."

Riley's fingers clenched and unclenched on the steering wheel, as she drove home. Erik and Frances had to be regretting their decision to let her get involved in their personal lives, considering Erik almost came to blows with Wayne. She never expected things to turn so ugly, nor have Wayne saying Frances might be in danger. She would never forgive herself if something happened to Frances, or the children.

Sharing Ian's data turned out to be like tossing a bomb in their midst. Riley expected they would want to go after Richard Melvin, not each other. She almost suggested Edward could be behind the secret account but changed her mind. Edward's motive would be resentment toward the family. Riley had an idea about someone else being the culprit, but she couldn't come up with that person's motive. She would have to leave town to get more info.

She caused a rift in the King family. She had to try to mend the crack before it widened any further. This phase would be done without Erik's permission. It may not be the wisest choice, but she couldn't just sit around waiting for Wayne and Erik to get at each other's throats again. She had started this and now it was up to her to seek out the answers to straighten things out.

THE LONELY ONES
Olivia Claire High

Riley remembered an incident when she was working at the bakery and she accidently dumped a huge pile of flour on the floor. Her father told her it was her responsibility to clean it up when she asked for help. He said a person needed to clean up their own messes, whether they be in the workplace or in life. The situation right now with the Kings certainly was a mess.

She called Erik and told him she decided to go to Hawaii for a few days and asked that he not contact her. He protested at first, but reluctantly agreed when she convinced him they all needed time to cool off after today's volatile meeting. Riley explained she hoped being away would soothe his family and a little beach time might help her to relax.

Well, at least the part about being near a beach was correct.

Chapter Nine

Riley pressed a hand to her jittery stomach, trying to build up the courage to enter the building. Her idea to do this seemed like a good plan at the time. But she began to doubt the wisdom of her impulsiveness now that she was standing in front of the place. Had she come all this way only to chicken out? A man carrying a gym bag came up behind her and held the door.

He lifted a brow when she continued to hesitate. "First time here?" Riley nodded. "Don't give up now," he smiled.

She thanked him, stepped inside Gerry's Gym, and entered Richard Melvin's world.

She hadn't been in many gyms, but this one looked very impressive. Light and airy with lots of machines and quite popular, if the amount of people working out meant anything. Thinking how Geraldine Melvin was murdered to make all this possible made Riley's stomach roll again.

Several people sat on stools at a long counter drinking what Riley assumed were health drinks. She wandered over to another counter where a slender young woman radiating health from her golden tanned body and shiny blonde hair to her perfect white smile.

"Hi, welcome to Gerry's Gym. May I help you?"

"I'm visiting and would like to exercise while I'm here. Can I get a limited membership?"

"Absolutely." She reached under the counter and drew out a brochure. "Here's a list of prices and the amenities the gym offers."

Riley took the folder and gave it a cursory glance. "Do you mind if I take a look around?"

"Oh, please do. And you are in luck because the owner is on site today. He enjoys giving guided tours of the facility to new people. I'll let him know you're here."

Riley would have nixed the idea, if her tongue didn't feel so thick in her mouth. She hadn't expected to come face to face with Richard this soon. Too late to turn back. The girl was already summoning him to the front desk. Riley's fingers tightened on the brochure, crinkling the pages when she saw him sauntering toward her. He'd bulked up even more since Erik's photo. Dark areas of sweat dampened his tank top, spotted his shorts, and glistened on his bare skin.

He held out a beefy hand. "Welcome to Gerry's," he said in a surprisingly soft voice.

Riley braced herself for his touch and pulled away as quickly as she could, wishing she could wipe her hand down the side of her shorts.

"Nice place you have here."

"We like to think so; and we pride ourselves on helping people to live a healthy lifestyle."

"Well, you certainly look to be in great shape yourself."

He punched a fist into his abdomen.

"You don't get abs like these by being a couch potato."

"No, I wouldn't think so. I'm visiting and thought I'd try to get in some workouts."

"Visiting, eh? Mind if I ask where from?"

"Alaska," she said, watching closely to see what his reaction would be, but his expression remained passive.

"Is that so? You're quite a long way from home. How are you liking Miami?"

"I like it fine, but I'm no stranger to a tropical climate. I was born and raised on Oahu."

"And you chose to move to Alaska?" He shook his head. "Now that's quite a transition."

She shrugged.

"It's just an experiment. I inherited quite a bit of money from my late father. I'm trying out different areas before I decide where I want to settle. I may even go back home."

Riley didn't miss a flash of greed in his eyes. Good. That was a reaction she needed to see. She deliberately told him she had money using it as bait to lure him into wanting to spend time with her. The next part of her plan would be to reveal she was looking for a way to protect her inheritance.

"So, how about that tour?" she asked, waving her hand toward the machines.

"It'd be my pleasure and I hope you will be impressed enough to spend some time with us while you are visiting. You look quite fit to me already. Do you have a regular exercise program?"

"Not really. I mostly just do some walking."

"Well, let's see if we can entice you to do a little more, shall we?"

"I'm all yours."

Yuk, did she really say that?

He smiled, revealing large teeth.

"Not yet."

Nausea swirled into her throat. Double yuk.

Riley swore her body ached to the point her muscles would be screaming if they had a voice. She could barely raise her arms to brush her hair without whimpering. Five days of workouts and she was tempted to give up her scheme to trap Richard. Who knew this was going to end up being so physically taxing? She may look fit, but appearances were deceiving in her case.

That was the bad news.

The good news was Richard made a point to see her every day. Riley took advantage of his attention and usually found a way to mention her money in their conversations. Almost a week of that and she knew it was time to move to the next phase of her plan by bringing up the subject of offshore accounts. She didn't want to stay away so long that Erik started calling her friends.

Riley told Richard she decided to leave in a couple days to visit her ailing godmother in another state. Her gamble paid off when he invited her to join him for lunch today. They entered what Riley's dad would have called a high-end restaurant. Tables covered with snowy white linen cloths, violins filling the atmosphere with soothing music playing softly in the background, and where a plate of dandelion greens cost fifteen dollars. The staff greeted Richard by name and lead the way to a table with a great deal of enthusiasm.

Richard raised his eyebrows when Riley sat down and purposely let out a long sigh.

"I hope that sigh didn't mean I've been working you too hard, or that you find I'm boring you."

"Oh no, I'm sorry about that. I received an annoying phone call right when I was getting ready to leave. This person has become a real pest, and I'm getting tired of the constant nagging."

"Must be pretty important to them if they won't leave you alone."

"They're making it about them. I asked for some advice on how to invest my money. It's appalling the amount of taxes I would have to pay. I'm told there are ways around that."

"Did they elaborate?"

"Hiding money in offshore accounts like in the Bahamas. I told them I don't want any trouble with the IRS. I doubt if anyone does that kind of thing anyway, except in movies."

"Actually, they do."

"Really?" she asked, giving him a wide-eyed stare with the naivety of a child.

"I have a friend who was forced to open an offshore account. I won't go into detail except to say he had to because he was being robbed blind tax wise. He suggested I do the same thing. I didn't, but at least I have the knowledge if I did ever decide to go that route."

How easily this man lied without showing an inkling that he was the so-called friend and the account was his. "Gee. Maybe they weren't kidding."

"What's this person's name who claims to have set up an account?"

"I'd rather not say. They did tell me the name on the account and said if I checked, their name would appear as the person who set it up. I assumed they were lying to impress me."

She sounded so ridiculous Riley couldn't believe he would take her seriously, but he did.

"Did you check to see if they were telling the truth?"

"I didn't even try. No one at any bank, let alone one with secret accounts would be willing to give me information like that. I mean, talk about impossible."

"Well, it wouldn't be impossible since you know the name on the account."

She fluttered her eyelashes. "Are you saying you could find out if such an account exists?"

"I could try," he said, pulling out his phone. "What name did they give you on the account?"

Now was the moment to find out if her theory was correct. Riley took a sip of water and almost choked in her nervousness.

"Frances Paige."

The jerk in his hand was so slight she probably wouldn't have noticed it if she hadn't been watching him like a hawk. He gave a great show of working on his phone. Riley gave him credit for putting up a smoke screen, but she knew he wouldn't be able to tell her who set up the account unless he already knew the answer.

He turned his phone, so she could see the screen. "Is this the person you've been talking to?"

Her water glass shook in her hand. "Yes."

Riley only managed a few bites of her lunch. If she had any doubts about Richard's involvement, he squashed them by showing her a name he couldn't have found if he didn't know it already. He went even further to encourage her to allow the friend to invest her money. No mystery there when she knew he would end up grabbing a big share for himself.

Riley left him as soon as she could, drove to her hotel, and barely made it to her room when her phone rang. Her first impulse was to ignore it, but a quick look showing Tessa's name made her take the call. She could use the sound of a friendly voice right now.

"Hi, how's the new mommy?" Riley asked, forcing a cheerfulness in her voice.

"More wonderful than I could have ever imagined. I can't wait for you to meet the baby."

"Speaking of babies, any update on Tanny's little one?"

"That's why I'm calling. She had her baby girl this morning and both are doing well."

"How wonderful! What did they name the baby?"

"They aren't sure yet. Tanny is leaning toward Robin, but Caleb isn't sure he likes that."

"He'll come around. At least she didn't suggest naming the baby Nene after the state bird."

"Good point. I may tell her to use that argument. How are you doing?"

"I'm, um, fine."

"Something is wrong. I can hear it in your voice. Is it your man? I know about his crash. Is he healing okay? Or is it something else? I hope he didn't dump you over Ian's information."

"Erik and I are still together and he's recovering okay, but his family is very upset."

"I suppose we shouldn't be surprised. I hope they didn't try to shoot down the messenger."

"Erik's brother-in-law wanted to for sure. He hates my guts right now."

"They need time to think things over. You may want to back off on researching for a while."

Riley made a face at herself in the mirrored closet door. "It's kind of late for such advice."

"I do not like the sound of that. What are you up to now?"

"I told Erik I was going to see you, but I came to Miami instead to see Richard Melvin."

Tessa gasped. "What! That's the guy Ian investigated. You did your own probing to know he is dangerous. Why did you deliberately seek him out? I can't believe you'd be so reckless."

"I had a hunch he would know who set up that offshore account Ian told me about."

"The Frances Paige one?"

"Yes. I was right, Tessa. I just got back from lunch with Richard, and he told me who did it."

"Riley, you are making me nervous. I understand you want to help Erik and his family get answers, but I doubt if they'd want you to put yourself in harm's way. I think you should get the heck out of there in case this guy decides your snooping may end up being trouble for him."

"I plan on leaving in the morning. Don't worry, I'm safe. He doesn't know my hotel. Do you mind if I end our call now and call Caleb to offer congratulations?"

"That's fine. They'll love hearing from you. Promise me you'll be careful."

"I will. Thanks for calling."

Riley talked to Caleb while Tanny was sleeping. She hung up after a few minutes and packed her suitcase. Her stomach rumbled letting her know she hadn't eaten much at lunch. She decided to go get the box of protein bars she left in her rental car. She walked out of her hotel and just reached the parking lot when she saw Richard looking in the windows of her car.

Tessa's warning rang in her ears. Riley spun around and ran the other way. She rushed to her room, grabbed her things and hurried out, avoiding the main entrance. Another hotel stood close by. She hustled over there keeping to the back near their parking area. She stayed in the shadows, sat on a bench, and started making reservations to change her flight.

She discovered she would have to take a night flight, but at least she could be out of Miami. She decided not to check out of her hotel or call about her rental car until just before she boarded the plane. No sense in doing anything to alert Richard she was leaving. She owed Tessa a call to tell her about the change in plans, but she wouldn't mention Richard being at her hotel. No sense piling on more worry. Riley was still sitting there with her phone in her hand when Tessa called her.

Tessa didn't bother with any greeting. "Listen to me, and do as I say. I told Ian what you've been doing, and you don't want to know his initial response. But once he calmed down, he said you shouldn't wait until tomorrow to leave. And when my husband gets that worked up about something, I know it's best to take his advice."

"You can tell Ian I just finished booking a flight for tonight after talking to you earlier. I'm dreading how Erik is going to react when I tell him where I've been."

"With good reason, but you have to tell him. Good luck. Let us know when you get home."

"It's going to be late," Riley warned.

"None of us here are going to rest until we know you're safe."

"I'm sorry, Tessa. I'll send you a text. Thanks for checking on me."

"Just get back to Erik. He's going to be happy to see you even if you did sneak out on him."

Erik might be happy to hear from her until she told him about seeing Richard Melvin. Perhaps it would be better to confide in him after she got home. The longer Riley sat there, the more she kept looking over her shoulder. What if Richard started scouting the bigger area for her? Calling a taxi to go to the airport right now, rather than waiting suddenly seemed like a good idea. She started to dig her phone out when she felt a presence behind her. Riley turned and came face to face with a woman holding a gun peeking out from beneath a jacket folded over her arm.

She never imagined Richard would send a woman to find her.

"We're going to the parking lot and don't forget my gun is pointed at your back."

"Please don't do this. Take my purse. I have money and credit cards. You can . . ."

"Shut up and move." She waved her hand at Riley's purse and bag.

"Bring those."

Clammy with nerves, Riley's entire body trembled, as she was forced to walk to the farthest corner of the lot until the woman stopped at a small sedan. She opened the trunk and pointed.

"Get in."

Chapter Ten

"You won't be in there long enough Riley's suitcase and purse slid from her numb fingers and fell to the ground.

"I'll suffocate."

I just need you to be hidden until I arrange a place for your lover to meet us. Then it's going to be showdown time."

"My lover?"

"Don't think you can fool me. I know you are Richard's latest girlfriend. I want him to see how it feels to lose someone he cares about."

Was this woman jealous that Riley was trying to steal her man? Time to straighten her out . . . or die trying.

"Wait, please. You couldn't be more wrong if you are under the impression that Richard Melvin is my lover. I would rather slit my wrists than be with that man."

"I don't believe you. I've watched you going into his gym every day and your cozy lunch together today. It's no use pretending that you aren't his latest conquest."

"I'm not pretending. The only reason I've been spending time with him is because I was trying to get information to help some friends of mine. I did enough research on him before I came here to believe he's the person behind some awful events involving them."

"What awful events? Who are you?"

"My name is Riley Hunter. I live in Juneau, Alaska. Richard lost his wife on a rafting tour there. I'm trying to prove it wasn't an accident."

"Are you talking about Erik King and his company ELK?"

Riley's eyes widened in surprise. "Yes. You've heard about them?"

"Oh, I've heard about them all right," she practically spat out the bitter words. "He's responsible for my sister's death."

"Oh my God," Riley muttered. "Are you Jacqueline, Geraldine Melvin's sister?"

"Jackie," she corrected. "If you know about my sister, then you know why I'm here. I tried to put her death behind me, but I just can't. Would you if you knew someone you loved died because of negligence? The accident happened because Erik King is a drug addict."

Riley waved her hands in front of her. "No, no, no, you couldn't be more wrong. It happened because Richard planned everything. Erik isn't an addict. He drank from a thermos of coffee Richard most likely drugged because he wanted Erik to be incapacitated."

"For what purpose?"

"I told you I researched Richard. I'm almost positive he intended to push your sister out of the raft that day, so he could collect the money from her life insurance policy to build his gym. He had to make it look like an accident and didn't want interference from Erik."

"Insurance? You're wrong. He built the gym with the money he got from suing ELK."

"That helped, but his main source of income over the years has come from him cashing in on the life insurance policies he takes out on his wives. That's how he builds his businesses."

"What other wives? What are you talking about?"

"I thought your sister would have told you. She was Richard's fourth wife."

Jackie staggered back a couple steps. "Fourth! That can't be. You're making all this up."

"I have proof. Didn't your sister tell you she wasn't Richard's first?"

"I don't think she knew, or she wouldn't have married him. How did the other wives die?"

"Supposedly by accidents and I found proof of that, too."

"Oh God. Oh God." A sob caught in Jackie's throat and she pressed fingers to her trembling lips. Her shock was genuine, the color draining from her thin cheeks, real. "I had a feeling he was no good. I begged Gerry not to marry him, but she wouldn't listen. He knew I didn't trust him, and he did everything he could to keep me away from her."

"Sounds like an isolate and conquer kind of strategy. Did you, um, start carrying a gun with you because you were afraid of Richard?"

"We had a huge argument the day of Gerry's funeral. He warned me to stay out of his life and I went away wanting to do something to get even with him."

Riley's brows arched.

"You bought a gun, so you could shoot him?"

"It belongs to a friend of mine, but I do know how to use it. I've been practicing. I don't think I would have the nerve to kill him, but I do want to see him be hurt."

"Do you think you could put it away now you know I didn't come here to be with Richard?"

Jackie stared down at the gun in her hand as though she'd forgotten it was there before she set it in the trunk. "I'm not crazy. I've just been going through a hard time. My sister and I were very close. Our father died when we were young. Mom is gone now, too. Gerry was the only family I had left, and Richard took her away from me."

"I'm so sorry. You've had it rough, and he sure didn't help to make things any easier."

"Now you know why I want him to suffer. He has to pay for what he's done."

"I agree and I think you could help me, but I don't want to put you in any danger."

"It shouldn't be a problem. We keep our distance, but he is used to seeing me around. I do live here, you know."

"If you're really interested in getting even with Richard you can keep an eye on him. I'm flying home tonight, but I'll leave you my number and we can stay in touch. What about the King family? I need to know if you are still harboring ill feelings toward them, especially Erik."

"I admit it will be difficult for me to have empathy for the man after hating him for so long."

"You have suffered a lot in losing your sister, but you should know Erik suffered a great deal, too. He had a breakdown after the river incident and became a recluse because he couldn't stop blaming himself. I'm not sure how many details you have about that day, but Erik did jump into the water to save your sister. He almost drowned in his drugged state."

Jackie closed the trunk and stood there shaking her head. "I didn't know any of that. Richard told me Erik King was on drugs and mishandled the raft so badly that's why Gerry fell out and drowned. Richard knew she wasn't a strong swimmer. I should have known better than to believe his lies."

"He's a murderer, Jackie. I'm going to continue researching him after I get home."

"I'll drive you to the airport, but I won't stay. You probably shouldn't be seen with me. You can't be too careful when it comes to Richard."

"I'm finding that out."

"I apologize for scaring you. It's just that I've waited so long to try and do something to make the pain Richard caused go away. But I was wrong to go after you. I don't want to . . . to hurt people. I'm not a mean person."

Riley squeezed Jackie's hand.

"It's okay, you didn't know anything about me. I really am sorry for the way Richard's cruelty has impacted your life."

"Not just mine from what you've told me." Jackie's hand clenched Riley's fingers so hard they both flinched.

"We have to stop him before he ruins more lives."

"That's why I came here."

They said their goodbyes at the airport with promises to keep each other in the loop. Jackie surprised Riley by hugging her. All in all, this had been a strange trip, and the results had only added more fuel to a conflagration that was already showing signs of being out of control. Bringing justice for the peoples' lives Richard Melvin had destroyed wasn't going to be easy, but she refused to give up. She thought of his unfortunate wives. He was a master of deceit and used their emotions to convince them to marry him.

They must have loved him when they married, but sadly love had cost them their lives.

Riley texted Tessa as soon as she got into her apartment. She flopped into bed with barely enough energy to get undressed. Most of her night was spent engulfed in nightmares about Richard coming after her. She woke up early hoping a shower would help. But the hot water did nothing to warm the chill that encased her body when she thought about how close she'd come to having Richard find her at her hotel. She couldn't stop shaking, and she shook even more when she thought about the call she must make to Erik. She probably was going to be in for some serious tongue lashing if his reaction turned out to be anything like Ian's.

She didn't know if it was a good sign or not when he answered on the first ring.

"I'm back."

"I don't think I could have stood another day not hearing from you. How was your trip?"

"Um, okay. Thank you for giving me the time I asked for without contacting me."

"It's one of the hardest things I've ever had to do given how upset you obviously were when you left here. I hope being with your friends has helped you to feel better."

Riley closed her eyes for a moment and prepared herself to rattle off her explanation, much as she did with Tessa, before she could lose her nerve.

"I wasn't with them, Erik. I went to Miami to see Richard Melvin, and try to find out what he knew about the *Frances Paige Account.*"

She waited for Erik's reply. He remained quiet, punishing her with his silence. Riley expected him to be angry with her, even disappointed, but never this absence of any emotion at all.

"Erik? Please say something."

"Are you safe now?" he asked in a voice taut with barely suppressed control.

"Yes. I'm in my apartment. I got home late last night. Do you want . . ."

Erik ended the call, cutting her off in mid-sentence. Riley pulled the phone away from her ear and stared at it.

He hung up on her. Now what? Her body sank down onto the sofa. It obviously was too late for regrets, but right at this moment she wished she hadn't listened to that nagging voice inside her head to get involved in this part of Erik's past.

But just as quickly the vision flashed before her eyes of him looking so miserable that night when he told her about the river accident and how it had nearly ruined his life. How could she forget the suffering Frances went through watching her brother's world slowly eroding away?

Riley tossed her phone onto the cushion next to her and bent forward and buried her face in her hands. Had she lost her own credibility while trying to find the truth for others? She found out what she needed to know by going to Miami, but Erik didn't appear to care what that something was. Would he ever trust her again? She stared at her silent phone.

Apparently not.

Her head jerked up at the sound of loud knocking at the door moments later.

"Let me in, Riley."

Erik! Her heart started beating in rhythm with his pounding. She looked toward the window thinking a quick jump would be better than having to face his wrath. Her pulse leaped and her hands shook, as she opened the door. Erik pushed his way into the room causing Riley to brace herself against the full brunt of his fury.

"Erik, I'm sorry. I know I should have . . ."

He snatched her into his arms, closed his mouth over hers, and unleashed the unbearable tension that had been building in them both since the phone call. Stunned, she put her arms around his neck and pressed herself closer. He wove his hands through her hair and deepened the kiss. The unexpectedness of his behavior filled Riley with such relief she parted her lips. A low, almost savage sounding groan escaped him.

Erik carried her to the sofa and cuddled her to his chest, a precious burden. She nestled against him, enjoying the unexpected reaction. He held her for several seconds, but disappointed her when he set her from him and rose from the sofa. His action reminded her too much of that time he did the same thing at his cabin. He stood, towering over her holding his body stiff, whether from their brief moments of passion, or a rousing sense of fury.

Probably the latter, Riley decided. She hadn't forgotten how angry he could be when riled.

"Do not ever go behind my back and do something so insanely stupid again," he ground out.

"You would have tried to stop me if I told you what I wanted to do. How is it stupid when I found out what you needed to know?"

He laughed without humor. "Oh, yes. The mysterious Frances Paige account that made you believe you were the only one who should go see a killer and have him explain about that."

"There's no need to be so sarcastic."

He shoved his hands into his pants pockets. "What the hell do you expect? You nearly gave me a heart attack saying you went to see Melvin. Are you trying to send me to an early grave?"

"No. I'm trying to save you from an early grave. I had the idea if you knew who set up the account you could find out why. I thought your dad did it, knowing how he resents your family."

Erik stared at the ceiling for a moment before looking at her again.

"Why am I not surprised? It sounds like something he would do just so he could cause trouble as usual. But to involve his own daughter is a lousy thing to do, even for him. Why didn't you just tell me?"

Riley cleared her throat.

"Erik, I said I thought it was your dad, but I was wrong."

"Okay, then, I assume it was Melvin. Fine. Now I know I need to watch my back."

"He's not the only person who is after your back."

"What do you mean?

"Wayne is the one who set up the account."

His eyes filled with something close to sympathy.

"Oh, Riley, I honestly don't blame you for wanting to get even with Wayne after the way he treated you, but going to such lengths by seeing Melvin was far too dangerous. He had to be lying if that's what he told you."

"I wasn't trying to get even with Wayne and Richard didn't tell me, he showed me."

"Whatever he showed you had to be fake. Those accounts are secret, Riley. That's why people have them. There is no way he could know such a thing."

"You're right, unless he already had the information. I never mentioned Wayne by name. I just said I had inherited quite a bit of money and a friend wanted to help me avoid taxes by setting up an offshore account in the Bahamas. I told Richard this friend gave me the name Frances Paige to prove that he knew what he was doing. Richard encouraged me to accept the offer to set up the account. Can't you see this is further proof he's involved? Richard wanted me to have Wayne put my money where he knew he could get his hands on it."

"Why would Wayne be involved with Richard Melvin, if what you say it true?"

"That I don't know. I guess you'll have to ask Wayne that yourself."

Wayne looked up when Erik entered his office. They hadn't been on the best of terms since Riley broke the news about the Frances Paige account. The set of Erik's jaw gave every indication this wasn't going to be a social visit.

"Erik, what brings you here?" Wayne asked, bracing himself for unpleasantness.

"I'd like some information from you."

"All right. Information about what?"

"I want to know why you're in contact with Richard Melvin and setting up offshore accounts for him," Erik asked, coming directly to the point of his visit.

"Wh . . .what are you talking about?" Wayne rasped, cowering at Erik's fierce expression.

"Cut the innocent act. You are in too deep for that ploy now. Tell me what's been going on between you and Melvin and do not insult me by trying to lie your way out of this."

"I didn't have a choice. He . . . he made me do it."

Erik quirked a brow.

"He made you do it? I see. And how did he go about that? Did he hold a gun to your head? Threaten you with bodily harm? Is that why you were so rude to Riley because she ripped into your charade?"

"No." Wayne licked his lips. "I mean, of course I didn't like it, but that's not what really had me so worked up. Richard said he would kill Frances and the boys if I didn't do what he wanted. That's why I was so upset with Riley's probing. Don't you see, she was signing their death warrant."

Erik's mouth gaped open.

"What!"

"It's true; and . . . and you helped her do it."

THE LONELY ONES
Olivia Claire High

Chapter Eleven

Erik stood in the doorway with his arms crossed over his chest when he entered the room. But now he reached Wayne in three strides and slapped his palms on the surface of the desk boxing Wayne in. He leaned so close Wayne pressed back against his chair.

"Richard Melvin threatened to kill Frances and the kids and you're just now telling me about it? What in the name of all that is holy made you keep such a thing to yourself?"

"Part of the threat demanded that I didn't tell you."

"Well you're going to tell me now by God, or I'm going to wring your scrawny neck."

Wayne's face paled. "Richard has photos on his phone he took of Frances and the boys."

"Photos doing what?" Erik demanded, narrowing his eyes.

"Frances going to work, dropping the kids off at school, the boys playing in the front yard. Things like that. He was here in town watching the house and following her."

"You should have told the police, threat or no and that would have been the end of it."

That . . .that wasn't the only threat he was holding over me." Wayne took a handkerchief out of his back pocket and began to mop at the beads of sweat covering his brow.

"I don't know what could be worse than him wanting to murder your family. But you may as well come clean about the rest."

"Okay, but please hear me out before you start throwing punches." He continued to wipe sweat away. "I was the one who tampered with your vest the day of the rafting trip."

Erik straightened up and glared at Wayne with such force the air practically crackled with his rage. "Melvin's the one jerking you around, but I'm the one you tried to kill. Nice to know you wanted me dead."

"I don't want you dead!" Wayne shouted, twisting out of his chair. "It was all part of Richard's scheme, so he could push his wife out of the raft."

Now Erik's face lost color.

"You knew he intended to kill her, and you let him go through with his murderous plot. Mrs. Melvin was the victim that day, but you're acting like it was you."

"I didn't realize his plan at first. He already showed me the photos of Frances and the kids and told me about his threat to harm them if I didn't foul up your vest. He took pictures of me doing it in case I tried to deny my part. I knew you were a strong swimmer, so I didn't doubt that you would survive even without the vest."

Erik snorted.

"With all that drugged coffee I drank. Yeah, right."

"I swear I didn't know anything about that. Richard must have put the drug in the thermos when I wasn't looking."

"You still haven't told me what all this has to do with the Frances Paige account. I want to know why you used that name. It's a little too close to home, wouldn't you say?"

"Richard insisted I use someone in the family. The best I could do to keep him from having me use the King name was to go with Paige. He made me set the account up, so he'd have a place to keep the money he demands I send to him."

"So, he's been blackmailing you all this time and you pay to keep your dirty secret."

"It's the only way I can make sure Frances and the boys will remain safe."

"Have you been skimming money off the company books?"

Wayne's jaw went slack, and he slumped back onto his chair.

"Yes, but how did you know? I've been very careful to hide it."

"Not careful enough. I know you did back off somewhat after I took over, but Frances suspected something was going on before. She chose not to tell you."

"She knows? I can't believe she never said anything to me."

"What if she had? Would you have told her about the stealing? Will you tell her now?"

"No. I didn't want to upset her. Can't we just let things go on the way they have been as long as she doesn't seem to be worried about it now that she's no longer in charge here?"

"Blackmailers aren't usually content with keeping things the same. Sooner or later they end up wanting more money."

"Richard's been okay with the status quo. I haven't given him any reason to believe I can't come up with the money."

"The man received enough money from us when he sued. You don't expect me to allow you to keep stealing from the company, do you?"

"How else are we supposed to keep Frances and the boys from harm?"

"They are the priority, but Melvin is going to be demanding more money from you."

Wayne's brow puckered in a frown.

"What makes you say that? I just told you he's been okay with what I've been sending him. I don't understand what you mean."

"I have a feeling you're about to find out pretty soon. If I'm right, he's going to expect you to skim a hell of a lot more off the books than you've been doing."

"Has Richard been threatening you, too? Is that how you found out I was the one who set up the offshore account? There wouldn't be any other way you could have known."

"It's enough that I know, and if he does demand more money you damn well better tell me."

"Who told you? I've confessed everything from my end. What more do you want from me? I would think my cooperation should give me the right to know who you've been talking to."

Erik walked to the door. "You lost your rights the day you began stealing from ELK."

"I told you I'm doing it to protect Frances and the boys."

"No Wayne, all you've been doing is helping the executioner sharpen his ax."

Erik went directly to Riley's apartment where he now paced.

"You were right all along."

"That's nice to know. But I feel as though I just walked in on the middle of a conversation. Care to tell me what part of whatever I said I was right about?"

"I'm talking about Wayne. He admitted he was the one who tampered with my vest."

Riley sliced her hand through the air. "I knew it! Why did he want you to die?"

"He claims he didn't. He knows I'm a strong swimmer and would have survived."

"After he drugged you? Oh, please! Talk about rationalizing to salve his conscience."

"Wayne insists he didn't go that far, and that Richard must have added the drug."

"I can believe that. But what about Mrs. Melvin? Did Wayne know ahead of time what Richard planned for her?"

"Yes, but apparently not at first. He claims he couldn't say anything because Melvin threatened to go after Frances and the kids if he did."

"Oh, Erik, I was afraid of that. We have got to get enough evidence to make sure Richard Melvin is locked away. I promised Gerry's sister."

Erik stopped pacing. "Mrs. Melvin's sister? When did you talk to her?"

"I planned on telling you before I got sidetracked with the information about Wayne. She lives in Miami. She thought I was Richard's latest lover. She pulled a gun on me and forced me to her car, but I straightened everything out, and we're on good terms now. In fact, she's going to keep a close eye on . . ." Riley stopped. "What's wrong? Why are you looking at me that way?"

"For God's sake, Riley, you just told me you were kidnapped at gunpoint

"Almost kidnapped, so there's no sense dwelling on it. It's better to turn a blind eye and a deaf ear to the incident. I told you we ended up connecting. Her name is Jackie and she's been suffering from losing her sister. She needs us. I promised to help her make Richard pay."

Erik took a hold of Riley's hands, brought them to his lips, and kissed her fingers.

"You could have been angry with this woman, but instead you want to help her. The fact that she tried to kidnap you could mean she's still holding a grudge, even though you say you bonded."

"I know what I say and do doesn't always jive with facts. But sometimes I think you have to forget the exact science of facts and just have faith."

"Are you talking about me having faith in Wayne?"

"Well, I wasn't when I said that, but we do have to have his cooperation. He's our link to Richard, and I bet Wayne would be happy to stop paying out blackmail money."

"I don't care about the money as much as I do about Fran and the kids being safe."

"Do you know how to do that, short of making them stay inside under armed guards?"

"I'll have to send them away."

"That means you are going to have to tell her about Wayne. How do you think she'll react?"

"Not very well, but I'll at least spare her the news about him screwing up my vest. The main thing is to get her out of here, so Melvin can't get his hands on her and the boys."

"Do you think it would help if I went with you when you talk to Frances?"

"I think it'd be easier for her if we keep the meeting between family. Besides, you're going to be too busy packing for your own trip."

"What are you talking about? What trip? I'm not going anywhere. I just got back to Juneau."

"You're going to Hawaii, and this time I'll be with you to make sure that's exactly where you end up."

Riley pulled away.

"Oh no you don't! I want to stay here to help you tie up Richard."

"The only person who will be tied up is you if you refuse. I nearly lost my mind when you told me you'd been in Miami with Melvin. I'm not going to put myself through that again in case you come up with another one of your wild ideas."

"I'll be good. Please let me stay," she promised, letting his criticism pass.

"No."

She gave him a shrewd look.

"You know, you won't be able to help catch Richard if you go with me to Hawaii."

"I'll be a delivery service only. I plan to leave as soon as you're settled."

"I'll . . . I'll tell my friends you're forcing me to stay. Who do you think they'll side with?"

"My guess would be the person who is trying to keep you from getting killed."

Erik ended his call to Ian Hawk. He dropped Riley off at their house almost a week ago and she was still grumbling about being taken out of the loop, according to Ian. But it sounded like he and their friend Caleb understood Erik's frustration with Riley after he listened to Ian describe how he and Caleb had gone through the same kind of argument with their wives.

Caleb called the women the three musketeers. Erik thought they sounded more like three vigilantes. But apparently the ladies had been quite helpful when the families were all going through a crisis of their own. He decided that might be a good thing to keep in mind. He sat down at his desk to do some work when Wayne burst into the room.

"You called in an auditor?" he demanded, his body literally shaking with anger. "I just heard from them. They're coming here. I can't believe you would do that. Why didn't you tell me?"

"I don't know why you would think I wouldn't. I would have had the books audited not long after I took over here if I wasn't so busy flying from site to site and dealing with problems in the other offices. Now there's too much information to let things go any further."

"Why are you stabbing me in the back like this?"

"I'm not stabbing you in the back. I'm trying to help you."

"I fail to see how having an outsider go over the company's books is going to help me."

"Melvin will want to know why when you stopped sending money. This is your out. Tell him I discovered discrepancy in the books and ordered an audit. He'll probably do two things."

Wayne ran fingers through his thinning hair.

"Yeah. Kill me and then go after Frances."

"He doesn't know Frances and the boys are in southern California with friends."

"What about me? I'm still here. He's probably going to come after me to get his money."

"That's what I want to happen because that's how we will trap him."

"Using me as bait. Thanks a lot! What two things did you mean Richard might do?"

"Threaten Frances and demand the extra money he thinks you're getting."

"Yes, what about that? What am I supposed to say to him?"

"Convince him you never got the money. He'll want to come here to collect his share in person. Say Dad mishandled things when he was boss, and the mistakes are just showing up."

"You aren't really going to go so far back, are you?"

"May as well, as long as I have the audit starting. Why do you care at this point?"

"I hoped I wouldn't have to tell you or Frances. You aren't going to believe me because I've sent money to Richard, but your father made me alter the books for him, too."

Erik's brow jutted up.

"So that's why you never wanted Frances to check finances."

"It's not like that," Wayne denied, licking his lips in a nervous little flick of his tongue.

"No? Then suppose you explain to me what it is like."

Chapter Twelve

"I admit I never wanted to tell you about Richard blackmailing me, but you don't know how many times I was tempted to explain what was going on with your dad."

"And you didn't because . . .?" Erik asked, arching another brow.

"You and Frances have already been hurt so much by Edward over the years I thought it would be best to spare you."

"Save your pseudo heroism for someone who cares. I want to know why you skewed the books for my father, or do I have to call him for an explanation?"

"You don't think he would cooperate, do you?" Wayne's lips tightened when Erik continued to pin him with his unrelenting stare. "Your father is addicted to gambling."

"Gambling?"

"Yes. He goes to Las Vegas several times a year."

"Is that so? You have proof of these trips?"

Wayne shook his head.

"No. He demanded I give him huge amounts of cash and then makes his own arrangements. I tried to find out where he stays, but he must use assumed names."

"How convenient for you both. What if Fran asked about the trips?"

"Edward told me to tell her they were for business mixed with pleasure and that he used them to drum up more business for ELK."

"Is he still asking you for money?"

"Not since Ernest kicked him out. That's why he keeps pestering Frances to get Ernest to increase his allowance."

"I happen to know my grandfather told you to give Dad an increase."

He waited, but Wayne didn't reply.

"You never told my father, did you?"

Wayne looked away, but Erik got a glimpse of bright color flooding his face.

"I . . ."

"Don't bother to deny it. My, my you have been a busy boy," Erik said with heavy sarcasm.

Wayne clenched his fists in anger, infuriated by Erik's arrogance.

"You're just like your grandfather. I put up with him every damn day telling me what a failure I am. I'll never be good enough to gain his approval, especially when he thinks you're so perfect. Go ahead, mock me. It's what you Kings do best."

"There you go, feeling sorry for yourself again. You'd be sitting behind bars if I were my grandfather. The only reason you're not is because I haven't told him about your unique brand of bookkeeping. I also don't want to hurt Fran."

"I did what I had to do with the books for your dad and what Richard made me do to your vest. I was forced to walk a fine line. I only wanted to make sure the family was safe."

"Uh-huh, and messing with my vest was supposed to keep me safe?"

"Damn it, Erik. What did you expect? I already told you I had to after Richard's threats."

"No, you didn't. What you should have done was tell me that day on the river, so we could have stopped him. His wife would be alive, and I wouldn't have almost died myself."

"Richard caught me off guard."

"Well, you damn well better start being on your guard now if we're going to stop him."

"You know, you have a lot of nerve sitting there lecturing me when you were the one who ran away and left Frances and me to keep things going here. Then you decide to return when it's convenient for you and get welcomed back like the proverbial prodigal son, despite your wasting all that time in that cabin of yours without a care to what was going on with the business."

"Convenient for you, too, without having me paying attention to your bookkeeping. And you're wrong when you said I don't care about the company, but you are right about me running away. I ran because I couldn't get over the fact that I was responsible for an innocent woman's death. The guilt of that broke me, which made me feel useless here. You could have prevented that if you told me about Richard Melvin's plot. Makes me wonder how you can stand knowing you should have stopped him. What about how you sat there when the judge awarded Melvin the money in the suit against ELK? Talk about adding insult to injury."

"Not a day goes by that I don't regret all that. You're lucky you have found peace within yourself. You have no idea what's it's been like having to live with all this inside my head."

"And I don't want to know. I've had enough trouble dealing with my own demons. We're done for now. Go back to your office and get ready to tell the auditor your secrets. You better hope to God my grandfather doesn't find out what you've been doing to his beloved ELK."

Wayne walked to the door and tightened his hand on the knob before he turned to Erik again.

"You've made it clear you think I'm responsible for letting Richard kill his wife. But who do you think gave him the idea to bring her on the rafting trip?"

"Richard, of course. That goes without saying."

Wayne snorted.

"It was your dad. He met Richard on one of his Vegas trips. So, you see between that and his gambling I'm not the only one with secrets around here."

Wayne entered his own office, slammed the door, and slumped onto the chair behind his desk. An uncontrollable surge of anger burst through him until he picked up his coffee mug and hurled it across the room. He threw the cup with such force it shattered into several pieces against the wall. It didn't matter that it had been a gift from his boys for last Father's Day. He was too furious to care, or to feel any sentiment right now.

He wasn't only burning with anger, but bitter humiliation at the way Erik treated him. Ernest was bad enough to deal with and now he had the added burden of being made to put up with Erik's arrogance as well. God, he was so like the old man sitting behind that big desk like it was a throne. Wayne got up to pace, ignoring the way his shoes crunched over the shards of broken pottery scattered around the floor.

How dare Erik ridicule him as though he was a criminal, even after he explained keeping Frances safe was the reason for skewing the books. Wayne had little doubt she would probably side with her precious brother. She was always defending him no matter what he did. But let him, her own husband make a mistake and he couldn't have any guarantee who would gain her loyalty. It galled him to know she had more admiration and respect for Erik than she did for him.

Oh, she did her best to hide her feelings, but he knew. He'd always known from the very beginning when they were at college together. His hands balled into fists. He was damn sick and tired of being made to eat Erik's dust. He was also aware that his children preferred their uncle to their own father. And speaking of fathers, Wayne knew he at least got in the last shot when he told Erik his dad was the reason Richard came to Alaska that fateful day.

The look on his brother-in-law's face almost made up for the sarcasm and indignity, he'd been forced to endure.

Almost.

He slid back onto his chair again.

Wayne had to find a way out of this situation if he was going to have any leverage at all. Didn't he have a right to protect himself? No one in their right mind would want to be a sitting duck. Yet, Erik expected him to hang around waiting to lure Richard here. Wayne rolled a pen between his fingers. What if Richard did end up demanding a large payment thinking there was extra money to be had? Erik seemed awfully sure that was going to happen. Wayne knew no amount of juggling the company's books would allow him to meet such a demand now that he'd confessed to his earlier modifying.

What really bugged Wayne was how Erik found out he was the person who set up the bank account. It didn't seem like Richard would be volunteering such information unless there was something in it for him and that something was obviously money. Who tipped Erik off? Wayne knew he wouldn't be in this predicament if the rafting incident hadn't suddenly become a hot topic of conversation. Strange when you think how the incident had been taboo for so long. But all it took was one nosy person digging around and now he was being forced into a corner

Who encouraged Erik to come back to work? Who made him believe Mrs. Melvin's death might not be an accident? Who brought in her friends to do research until they found out about the Frances Paige account? Riley Hunter. The woman who was responsible for turning his life upside-down. Wayne wrote the name on a pad.

He drew a line through it tearing the paper with the heavy pressure he exerted on his pen. Then he waded up the paper and tossed it into the trashcan by his desk. How nice it would be if a person could get rid of people you didn't want in your life so easily.

Wayne wasn't the only one seething in anger at Erik's high-handedness. Riley was doing her own pouting several thousand miles away. She understood that he wanted her to be safe, but she didn't enjoy sitting around when she really wanted to help. Hadn't she already given him important information? He wouldn't have the answers he had right now in this complicated situation if it wasn't for her being willing to stick her neck out.

And what thanks did she get? Abandonment. Well . . . kind of.

Riley realized when she wasn't stewing with anger that she was being unfair to think such a thing. Erik was doing what he thought was best. He did make love to her the night before he went back to Alaska and showed her just how much she meant to him with not only his body, but also with his words. He confessed again how shaken he was when she told him about her trip to Miami. She knew that took a lot for a man with his pride to admit a weakness.

But she also knew if she was his weakness, he was hers. The knowledge of those feelings could be a powerful tool in the hands of someone like Richard Melvin who wouldn't hesitate to use that against them. All he would have to do was get a hold of one of them and Richard would have the upper hand. The other would surely do anything Richard asked of them.

So, here she sat in Hawaii, while Erik stayed in Alaska.

It wasn't as though Riley didn't enjoy being with her friends. Just seeing Tessa and Ian when they came to the airport to meet them had Riley practically running into her friend's outstretched arms as soon as she saw Tessa. Her wonderful friend glowed with the radiance of new motherhood. Ian stood back and waited before Riley introduced them both to Erik.

Curiosity made her pay close attention to see how the two men would react to each other. She knew they'd talked on the phone, but to see them in person would be the true test of how they would accept each other. She worried how Erik would relate to Ian considering Ian was the one who found out about the Frances Paige account in his research.

She watched the two alpha males with powerful personalities quickly sizing each other up during their brief handshake. Riley almost breathed a sigh of relief when these two important men in her life smiled and clapped each other on their shoulders.

They left the airport for Caleb and Tanny's house where Riley enjoyed a wonderful reunion with them and got to meet their new baby girl, Robin. Riley paid close attention again hoping these other two strong men would hit it off as well as Ian and Erik seemed to be doing.

Turned out she needn't have worried. Caleb offered beer, and the three of them went outside, so the ladies could have their girl time alone. Tessa and Tanny showed their own approved of Erik by teasing Riley about landing such a hunk. She didn't object to their humor, considering they were married to a couple of sexy men themselves.

They ended up all having dinner at Ian's and Tessa's house and talking late into the night. Neither Erik nor Riley brought up the reason she would be staying here, but she knew much had been discussed via phone calls while plans were being made before she even boarded the plane. She tried not to let that bother her.

Riley loved being able to spend time with Tessa and Tanny and their adorable babies, but she still wanted to know how Erik was handling Wayne. She tried prying information out of him by asking how she was supposed to keep Jackie in the loop if she wasn't given updates, but he continued to avoid answering her questions during their telephone calls.

She'd been away for several days now and as much as she tried to control her feelings of anger her restlessness made her want to be more actively involved again. She promised Erik on every phone call she would be careful if he would let her return to Alaska, but he remained adamant that he wanted her to stay put.

Erik did point out Jackie's only real defense against Richard was for her to continue to act ignorant on how her sister really died. It was important Richard never found out the two women met. Riley called to tell Jackie that Erik insisted she stay in Hawaii without any promise to keep her informed on how events were progressing. Jackie expressed her disappointment at this latest development. She also said she received a call from Richard inviting her to join his gym at no cost. He acted surprise that she hadn't come sooner saying he felt sure Gerry would want her to.

Jackie told Riley she hadn't decided what to do yet because she was so furious with Richard now that she knew he was the one responsible for her sister's death. That had Riley worried Jackie might get reckless and say too much to Richard in a fit of frustration. She begged Jackie to be very careful about letting anything slip about them meeting.

Riley understood how Jackie felt. The woman hated Richard and her wish for revenge had almost become as strong as the love she had for her sister. Riley didn't want to make a pest of herself, but a sense of unease continued to nag at her until she decided she would give Jackie a quick call each day to check that everything was okay.

She explained it was something she had to do for her own peace of mind. Jackie seemed to understand Riley's concern and agreed to accept the calls. Everything went fine for the next few days. The conversations were brief, but at least they were keeping in touch until Riley made her usual call and found out Jackie's number was no longer in service. She told herself not to think the worse. Jackie probably just decided to change numbers and would be letting her know very soon. But after another day passed with no word, Riley was convinced something bad had happened. She felt helpless being so far away. The only thing she could think to do was alert Erik. He had more resources available to him if Jackie was going to need help.

"I'm afraid Richard has Jackie," Riley blurted, as soon as Erik answered her call.

"What makes you think that?" Erik asked, his voice calm.

"We've been talking daily, but now her number is out of service and she hasn't given me a new one. She said

Richard asked her to join his gym. That seems strange to me after the way they argued at her sister's funeral. I'm wondering why he suddenly wants to see her on a regular basis. I warned her to be careful. She may not be able to control her temper now that she knows he's responsible for her sister's death. I'm worried she had it out with him, and he's done something to hurt her. I don't want to go behind your back this time. I'm telling you upfront I've decided to go to Miami and find out if Jackie is all right."

"Think again."

"No, you think again, buddy. This isn't just about me. I want to know if she's okay."

"I doubt you think of me as your buddy right now. But to ease your fears, Jackie is fine."

"How can you be so sure?"

"Because I know where she is."

Chapter Thirteen

"Why didn't you tell me?" Riley asked, forcing her anger down. "Why didn't Jackie let me know what's going on? I'm getting tired of being treated like someone who can't be trusted."

"Calm down. I told her not to contact you. I planned on calling you tonight. I had to wait until all the details were worked out."

"What details? Where is Jackie?"

"In a safe place. I told Caleb and Ian when I was with them there was some concern Melvin may start paying closer attention to Jackie. Caleb asked his friend to keep an eye out for her."

"Is he the guy who helped when we were trying to find out about the offshore account?"

"One and the same. He's been following Jackie. She did end up going to the gym and meeting with Richard. He also noticed Richard started to follow Jackie. Ken called Caleb and Caleb called me. We agreed Melvin could be up to no good, so Ken convinced her to get out of Miami. She decided to stay in a bed and breakfast inn owned by friends in Rhode Island. Ken is driving her there, and we advised her not to get in touch with you until she was settled."

"Is she going to get a new phone number and give it to me?"

"Yes, and I want you to get a new one too, but don't use your name. We don't want there to be any way

Melvin can trace your calls. He may have been checking on Jackie's phone already."

"I never thought of that. I'll get a new number, but then Jackie won't be able to call me."

"I'll make sure you both exchange numbers as soon as I have them. We are taking this one step at a time to ensure the safety of everyone. Melvin is becoming suspicious that something is going on. He's going to be paying more attention to any activity involving him."

"I'm in Hawaii. You're in Alaska. Frances is in California, and Jackie is heading for Rhode Island. We're scattered all over the map because of what one man may or may not do. I appreciate you trying to keep us safe, but we can't stay away forever, you know."

"I realize that, but we won't have to wait much longer for things to come to a head. Wayne's payment to Melvin is coming due. He isn't going to sit back and do nothing when Wayne tells him he refuses to pay, especially if he thinks you gave Wayne all your money."

Riley blew out a whistle.

"That's going to put Wayne in the danger zone big time."

"Nothing he hasn't already caused to happen to himself."

"You don't sound very sympathetic. Not that I blame you, considering what he's done."

"It's difficult to have sympathy for a man who could have had me killed," Erik snapped.

"I'm sure. How are you and Wayne getting along now that Frances isn't there as a buffer?"

"I'm not exactly his favorite person right now, nor is he mine."

"Does your grandfather know what's going on? He has to suspect something with Frances and the boys leaving without any date to return home."

"He knows enough to make him dislike Wayne even more than he did before, but we're all doing our best to tolerate each other for my sister's sake."

Riley rolled her eyes.

"Good lord. It must be hell living in that house right now."

"It is, but I have to stay to keep an eye on Wayne."

"I bet you wish you were staying at your cabin."

"The only good memory I have of that place is when I had you with me there."

"Thank you for saying that," Riley said, her tone going soft with emotion.

"It's true. I miss being with you now. We have to hope things won't go on much longer, so we can be together again."

"I suppose you still won't tell me what your plans are," Riley asked, hoping he would.

"My plans depend on what Melvin decides to do when he doesn't get his money."

"I suppose so. Well, please be careful and don't forget to watch your back."

"I intend to and be sure to watch your own, as well," Erik warned.

"Why would I have to do that?"

"I'm just reminding you to be conscious of your surroundings, and to be alert for anything that seems out of the ordinary."

"You sent me here, so I wouldn't have to watch my back. Besides, Ian and Caleb are watching it for me. I can barely walk out the door without one of them or Tessa and Tanny asking me where I'm going."

"We all want to keep you safe."

"I know and I do appreciate your concern, but we don't have to worry about Richard because he doesn't know where I am."

"True, but Wayne knows you aren't at work and he may end up remembering you came from Hawaii and have friends there he now despises. He was quite sore with you about the Frances Paige account, and he's angry enough with me right now to take his temper out on you."

"He's already in so much trouble, why would he want to make things worse for himself?"

"I imagine he's feeling since he's such a black sheep, he doesn't have much to lose. He may try to do something that makes him feel better, especially if it means he can get even with me."

"Then I may as well come home."

"That would only make it easier for him to get to you. It's better if you stay put where Ian and Caleb can keep an eye on you. They know I have enough on my plate having to watch and wait to see what Wayne will do and if Melvin will strike. I can't afford to have you get caught in the crossfire."

"Okay, I get it," she breathed out a long sigh. "He will hurt you if he hurts me."

"Big time."

"Love and hate are such powerful emotions."

"Yes, and either one can bring a man to his knees."

"Women, too. I love you, Erik King."

"And you are my heart, Riley Hunter."

Riley missed Erik terribly. She supposed it wasn't a surprise that she had a very vivid dream about him that night after their conversation. A wonderful dream filled with sweet words of passion and endless hours of shared bliss. Riley reveled in the taste of his mouth and the touch of his hands roaming over her naked body. She smiled until her lovely dream suddenly turned ugly.

Wayne materialized out of the shadows coming toward her with eyes blazing in anger. Where was Erik? She looked around instinctively wanting his protection. She tried to call for him but ended up gasping out a shocked breath that jolted her awake. She scooted to sit up in bed feeling sick with fear wondering for a moment if Wayne really had come into her room.

Richard painted him in a corner with his back to the wall. Erik offered him an out by cooperating in capturing Richard. But Riley worried that Wayne might hate Erik even more than he disliked Richard. All this pressure could make Wayne strike out to defend himself.

Riley clutched her stomach knowing she was also responsible for Wayne's secrets coming to light. She couldn't forget that everyone in the King family had been trying to move on with their lives until she came along and started stirring up things about Geraldine Melvin's death. The sordid details started coming out one by one until they were now in the current situation.

Erik said Wayne hated him right now. Well, he must positively despise her. No wonder Erik warned her to be extra careful. She was safe staying in Hawaii with people who knew how to look out for people they cared about. The thought of Wayne or Richard coming after her here was remote. But with people being able to hack into computers and phones to find information her travel plans coming here wouldn't exactly be a secret.

A quivery breath escaped her thinking about the way Wayne looked at her when he demanded she be fired from ELK. Riley also couldn't forget how Richard ended up circling her car at the hotel that day. That probably meant he must have started to have his doubts about why she came to Miami. Then there was Jackie to think about. She'd been okay keeping her distance until Riley told her Richard pushed Geraldine out of the raft.

Once again, Riley began to worry she had caused too much damage in her honest desire to try and help people. She tried to give herself a pep talk. Sometimes when you discovered bad things, good things could end up coming from them, couldn't they?

Or was it the other way around?

Riley leaned over, switched on the bedside lamp, pulled her knees up to her chest, and rested her forehead on them. Part of her wished she had never started all this, but there was no turning back now. The stage had been set, and the drama must play out. The principal characters would soon all come together and do their parts. Riley promised Erik she wouldn't be there. Not even in the audience where she once thought she would have been invited to a front row seat.

She'd be okay with that if she didn't think she was entitled to be there, but her promise to Erik to stay here kept getting in the way. It wasn't that she wanted to deliberately put herself in danger. It was more that she still felt she could be of use to him. Riley didn't blame Erik for not trusting Wayne. Why would he after all the things Wayne had done to the family? Too bad Erik had to rely on his brother-in-law to draw out Richard and having to juggle two nemeses.

A soft tap at the bedroom door diverted her attention.

"I saw your light was on. Are you okay?" Tessa asked, keeping her voice low.

Riley jumped out of bed and hurried to open the door. "I'm fine. I'm sorry I woke you."

"You didn't." She tugged at the front of her robe. "I was nursing the baby. He's back in his crib asleep now. Do you need to talk, or would you rather I leave you alone?"

Riley stepped back, inviting Tessa to come in. "I could use some company if you're sure you don't need to go back to bed right now yourself."

Tessa sat on a chair.

"I'll sleep later. What's wrong? Are you thinking about Erik?"

Riley sank down onto the bed.

"Who else? You know I love being with you guys, but I'm lonely for Erik, and I'm also concerned for him."

"He didn't send you here to sit up worrying about him like this, you know."

"I know, but I can't help it. I've been mulling over some troublesome thoughts. What if Richard and Wayne decided to ban together and turn on Erik just so they can save their own skins. Erik is so concerned about protecting me, but who will be there to watch over him if the very guys he's trying to snare, end up pulling a fast one?"

"Well, I don't think that's likely if Wayne really wants to escape Richard's clutches. Erik told Ian and Caleb Wayne knows he can't keep paying out the money like he's been doing."

"Yes, but what if it becomes more about him hating Erik than it does about the money? His animosity has probably been growing the more time that goes on."

"I doubt if he'd do anything to harm Erik knowing how much Frances loves her brother."

"That's part of the problem. Wayne is jealous of Erik. He may be tempted to do something too drastic."

Tessa frowned.

"Are you thinking Wayne might try to stage another so-called accident?"

"Wouldn't you if you were in his shoes?"

Chapter Fourteen

Wayne massaged his temples working his fingers around and around in small circles. The pressure building in his head made him feel his brain might explode any minute. Was it any wonder the way people were coming at him from all sides with their demands? Richard's threatening calls and text messages insisting Wayne was sitting on a pile of money and holding out on him. Erik breathing down his neck pushing him to get Richard to come here. Now a call from Frances nagging him about when she and the boys could come home. He almost told her she didn't know how lucky she was to be away.

He could reason with Frances by playing on her sympathies, but Richard and Erik were different entities altogether. He hated to admit just how much they both intimidated him. If only he could think of a way to make them stop hounding him. They were both physically strong men while he'd always had to rely more on his mental abilities. Wayne could easily imagine them as gladiators facing each other in an arena fighting to the death.

It truly amazed him that Richard Melvin was still walking around without a scratch on him, considering how many people the man had conned and killed. He just hadn't been caught. Yet. But Erik's story was entirely different. He came back to the office and was greeted like a beloved king returning from exile. People may have gossiped about him after the river incident, but it didn't take long for that special charisma he seemed to possess to win everyone over.

Well, not actually quite everyone now that Wayne thought about it. What about the speculation that Erik's plane crash may not have been an accident? Could it really have been an attempt on Erik's life? Who disliked his brother-in-law enough to want him dead, and would they try again? Wayne sat in his chair, leaned his head back, and closed his eyes. What would it mean to him personally if Erik wasn't around watching his every move and forcing him to answer for practically the air that he breathed?

One word came to mind.

Freedom.

A sudden fierce thumping of his heart began to join in rhythm with the pounding inside his head, as he remembered something. The broken mug reminded him of the shattered wreck his life had become. He could sit here wallowing in bitter regret torturing himself or try to change his status. Some things you thought couldn't be mended might be fixable if you had the right tools . . . and the right people to help you.

The mug reminded him of how smoothly maintenance cleaned it away. Maintenance guys could be handy.

Wayne received a call on his cell phone a couple of days later as he sat eating dinner with Ernest and Erik.

Ernest looked up and glowered.

"I thought I told you to shut that damn thing off when we're having a meal."

"I know that, but this is a call I should take. Excuse me."

"Is it from Frances?" Erik wanted to know.

"No," he said and picked up his pace, leaving the room as quickly as possible.

Ernest looked at Erik. "What do you suppose that was all about?"

"Who knows? Wayne does have a life outside of this house and his office at ELK."

"Can't be much of a life the way he's screwed up. Reminds me of my worthless son."

Erik turned his attention back to his own meal and wisely did not reply.

Wayne knocked on Erik's bedroom door early the next morning.

"I need to talk to you before you go to work. It's about that phone call I received last night."

Erik stepped back so Wayne could enter the room and shut the door.

"Was it from Melvin?"

"No. I'm beginning to think he's planning on showing up here unannounced."

"We'll be ready if he does. So, what's all the mystery about your phone call?"

"It was Arthur. He called me to say his granddaughter died."

Erik's eyes clouded in a reaction of genuine sorrow.

"I'm sorry to hear that. I haven't seen her since she was a little girl, but I know she and Art were close. How did she die?"

"I don't know, but Arthur was the one who found her. He's not taking it very well. He called me again and sounded very shook up. I tried to comfort him, but I don't think I did much good."

"Poor Arthur. I'll go talk to him. I'm surprised he didn't call either my grandfather or me."

"He said he didn't want to burden you with his problems. I don't know why he called me, since we've never had a close relationship. But I came to talk to you right now because I received a text saying he was heading to your cabin to . . . to commit suicide."

Erik struck Wayne with a razor shape stare.

"Jesus! I wouldn't have expected him to break like that. He's always been such a tough old guy."

"Yeah, well, sometimes it's the tough ones who fall the hardest."

"We can't just ignore this."

"That's why I thought I'd better tell you. I'm hoping he's bluffing about wanting to kill himself. Maybe he just needs to talk to someone? I thought of telling Ernest, but you know he's not much on dishing out sympathy. Arthur has always been very fond of you, so you could be the best person to try and console him."

"My first instinct is to rush out of here and find Arthur. But the last time I went to someone's aid I ended up in a plane crash because the message I received was phony," Erik said, cocking his head at Wayne.

Wayne's face flushed and his nostrils flared.

"I know what you're getting at, given the dynamics of our relationship right now, but I'm not making this up." He shoved his phone at Erik.

"Here's Arthur's last text. You can try to call him, but I already have and there's no answer. You know as well as I do you can't get a signal at your cabin."

Erik looked at the message and swore. "Okay, I'll go to the cabin and see what I can do." He handed Wayne's phone back and yanked opened his closet door where he pulled out a backpack. "I'll take a change of clothes in case I end up staying overnight. There are still some canned goods, so we'll have something to eat if it comes to a longer stay."

"Now that I think about it, I hope I didn't make a mistake in telling you all this even though I do believe you probably are the best person to be with Arthur. Promise me you won't do anything to yourself. You know Frances would be saying the same thing if she was here."

"What are you talking about?" Erik asked, looking up from stuffing clothes into his pack.

"I'm talking about how depressed you were while you were at the cabin. Going back might stir up bad memories, especially if you're dealing with a man who is talking about killing himself. Maybe I should go instead of you."

Erik shook his head.

"We just discussed that. I'm the most likely person to help him."

"Are you sure? Frances would never forgive me if you ended up doing something to yourself, and she found out I was the one responsible for sending you there. Perhaps you shouldn't go. We can always send someone else."

"We're not going to send anyone else and I'm not going to do anything to myself. I see no need to explain any of this to Frances. I'm going to hope that I can smooth things over for Arthur and bring him back. I might even suggest he come and stay with us here, so he won't be on his own. He's probably feeling pretty raw and is just trying to work through his grief right now."

"What if Frances hears about this? What do I say to her?" Wayne began to wring his hands.

"For God's sake, man, do you always make a decision and then analyze it to death? Frances is your wife, not your nanny. She won't know anything about Arthur unless you say something."

"I don't plan to."

"Then you have nothing to worry about. Arthur has been with ELK for too many years for me to ignore the fact that he's hurting and needs help. I can't just leave him to his own devices."

"Okay, but . . . but Arthur supposedly took a gun with him."

"I'm gratified by your concern for my well-being, but if I was in danger of turning a gun on myself, I would have done it when I spent all that time at the cabin on my own. I'm not going to shoot myself, so lighten up."

"What if Arthur turns the gun on you?"

"He won't. Now I'd like you to go and keep my grandfather occupied while I sneak away without him seeing me. Otherwise, he'll want to know what I'm doing carrying a backpack."

Wayne turned at the door.

"Please let me know as soon as you can how things are."

"I will."

"Give me a couple minutes to distract Ernest before you leave. Good luck."

"Thanks, and don't look so worried. I'm sure everything is going to work out all right."

"You just make sure you come back in one piece. I don't want to even think about how Ernest and Frances would handle it if something should happen to you, Erik."

"Relax, I assure you I'm not the wimp I was when I stayed at the cabin before."

Wayne knew he promised not to tell Frances about the situation, but he hadn't promised to keep Riley in the dark. He waited until he got to his office and called her. He had to leave a message asking her to phone him as soon as possible. He waited for a couple hours and decided to try her again when she didn't answer. Wayne supposed she wasn't going to get in touch because they hadn't exactly parted on the friendliest of terms. He phoned her again and this time he told her he was very concerned for Erik.

If that didn't get her attention, he didn't know what would.

Riley called him within two minutes of the last message, which convinced Wayne she had been sitting there avoiding his other call just as he'd suspected.

"What is this about Erik?" she asked without so much as a hello.

"I realize we don't like each other very much, but I'm willing to put my feelings aside long enough to tell you about my concerns and I hope you will hear me out."

"That all depends on what those concerns are about."

"I told you I'm calling about Erik."

"What's going on? And before you answer you should know I can't make Erik put you in his good graces."

Wayne pressed his lips together and gripped the arm of his chair.

"I'm not calling to ask you to fight my battles for me. We received a call this morning that Arthur, he's the. . ."

"I know who he is. ELK maintenance."

"Well, then maybe you also know he's been with ELK for years and the King family think of him as a friend."

"Yes, I know that, too. Are you calling to tell me something happened to Arthur?"

"Something hasn't happened yet, but he is definitely in a bad way. His granddaughter just passed away and he's so devasted he is threatening to commit suicide."

"I'm very sorry to hear that, but I don't understand what that has to do with Erik."

"Arthur went to Erik's cabin to shoot himself. Erik decided he should go there and try to talk Arthur out of it. I'm worried about Erik going back because it might throw him into a flashback. He still carries around a lot of bad memories from the time he spent there."

"Then why did you let him go, for heaven's sake?"

"I tried to stop him. I even told him I didn't think it was a good idea, but he insisted he would be fine."

"Does Frances know about any of this?"

"No and Erik made me promise not to tell her in case she decided she should come back here. He didn't want Ernest to know, either. So, you see, you're the only person I could think to call and express my concerns. I wanted to go instead of Erik, but neither of us thought I would be much help. Arthur's much closer to Erik than he's ever been to me."

"Do you truly believe Erik would actually hurt himself? I mean, he's been doing so well for quite some time now."

"You never saw what shape he was in during those early days after he fled to the cabin. He refused to get any help or even let us visit him there. He was burying himself while he was alive. He only came back to the house once in a great while and each time he left we thought it would be the last time we'd ever see him alive. I'm concerned that this might pull Erik back into the vortex of his own depression, while his goal is to try and talk Arthur out of his emotional turmoil."

"Now you really have me worried, but I don't know what I can do being . . ." Riley stopped, remembering she wasn't supposed to tell Wayne where she was.

"I know Erik wanted it to be a secret, but I figured out on my own that you went to your friends in Hawaii. Am I right?"

"Yes, as long as you did put two and two together."

"Don't worry, your secret is safe with me. Would you consider coming here, so we could both go to the cabin to be sure Erik is okay?"

"Erik told me not to leave here until he came for me."

"I understand that, but how can he come for you when he's busy going to Arthur? You can always go right back to Hawaii after we find out Erik is all right."

"But what can we do since he's already on his way there?"

"Well, better late than never. He may even welcome some help talking to Arthur."

Riley bit her lower lip.

"I'm not so sure about that. Erik might be peeved. He was very emphatic that I shouldn't go back to Alaska until he told me Richard was no longer a threat."

"None of us have heard from Richard in several days. He doesn't have to know you are coming back. I'll meet you at the airport myself, and we'll go directly to the cabin from there."

"It makes more sense that you go without me because you're closer."

"True, but I doubt if I would be able to do much good on my own if Erik does flip out. I don't want his blood on my hands. Do you?"

"Of course not. All right, I'll call you back when I have my travel information."

"Thank you. Hopefully, you'll be able to get a flight okay."

"I'm sure I will. My biggest problem is getting away without my friends trying to stop me."

"Make your reservations, tell them you're going shopping, and don't let them know where you are until you board the plane. No luggage. I'll bring you clothes from Frances's closet."

"Okay, that should work. I feel terrible deceiving my friends, though."

"I'm sure you would feel a lot worse if Erik ended up killing himself."

Chapter Fifteen

Ian ended his phone call, as Caleb entered the office.

"Got a minute?"

"Yes. I assume you're here about Riley."

"I take that to mean you heard she's headed back to Alaska."

"Yes. I just got off the phone with Tessa. She had no idea what was going on. Riley told her she was going shopping when she left the house. Tessa didn't have any reason not to believe her, considering Riley only carried a purse."

"She called Tanny while she was boarding the plane. I'd say that was planned, so we wouldn't be able to go to the airport and stop her from leaving."

"I don't understand why she's skipping out when Erik explicitly told her to stay put," Ian said, waving Caleb to a chair. "Tessa tried to get it out of her, but Riley said she had to hang up. She did say Riley mentioned really missing Erik. Do you suppose Erik got in touch with her?"

Caleb sat down and crossed one ankle over a knee.

"No, but his brother-in-law did. Tanny managed to get out of her that he called to say Erik was heading to his cabin to save a friend from committing suicide. Supposedly, Wayne is worried Erik will have a flashback and end up shooting himself."

"A flashback, huh? Erik seemed stable enough to me. I'm not inclined to believe the brother-in-law after the things Erik told us about him. What does his wife have to say about it?"

"Riley told Tanny not to call Frances because it would be too upsetting."

"What's upsetting is the fact that Riley is going back without Erik's knowledge. Call me suspicious, but I'm not buying the brother-in-law's story. I bet he has something planned when he sees Riley. This could be his petty way of getting back at Erik."

Caleb's eyes sharpened with interest.

"What kind of plan?"

"I don't know, but I'm sure it will be something unpleasant. Erik didn't trust Wayne and I'm thinking we shouldn't either."

"My sentiments exactly. Tanny checked and found out Riley's going to change planes in Seattle. I thought I could catch her there, but everything I found would arrive too late. I have a bad feeling about this, and it bothers me that we promised Erik to keep Riley here."

"I'm with you. Help yourself to a bottle of water if you'd like while I make a quick phone call," Ian said pointing to a mini refrigerator setting in one corner of the office.

"I hope that means you have a plan of your own," Caleb said, as he stood up.

"I do have an idea, and I'm about to find out if it will turn into a plan."

Ian made his call while Caleb stood looking out the window and tipping the bottle to his mouth for long swallows. Ian talked for a few minutes and pushed back from his desk.

"Okay, we're all set."

"Set for what?"

"I had a meeting this morning with a CEO whose company is based in Seattle. He's leaving via private jet today. I asked if we could hitch a ride. He said he'd be happy to have our company. We must leave for the airport right now, though. It will be faster if I drive rather than take the time to arrange for a ride. Call our wives and tell them we won't be home for dinner tonight. Erik gave me his grandfather's phone number. I'm going to call him. I'd be willing to bet he doesn't know anything about this."

Caleb tossed the plastic bottle into a trash can and clapped Ian on the shoulder.

"Damn, I can't believe you got us a way out of here so easily. Do you have a magic wand hidden under your shirt?"

"Just lucky with the timing and circumstances of another man's travel schedule."

"I think I love you," Caleb joked, as they took long strides out of the office.

"Please, I'm a married man."

Riley's mouth gaped open, and she stumbled back a couple steps, as Ian and Caleb walked up to her. "Wh . . .what are you two doing here?"

"Oh, we just happened to be in the neighborhood," Ian told her.

"But how is it possible that you got here ahead of me?"

Caleb jabbed a thumb toward Ian.

"Never underestimate Mr. Resourceful Man."

"I'm not going with you if that's why you came," she said, jutting her chin in the air.

"Two against one, sweetheart and I hate to break it to you, but we're bigger than you."

"Caleb, you don't understand. I have to make sure Erik is going to be all right."

"Oh, come on, Riley. You know very well he was fine when he left you in our care."

"Things may change. People sometimes have flashbacks years after experiencing emotional trauma; and from everything Frances and Wayne told me, Erik was in a very bad way for a long time. I would never forgive myself if something did happen to him. Please, I'm begging you don't deny me the opportunity to see for myself that he really is going to be all right."

"Wayne's an ass," Caleb said. "But you are right about flashbacks."

"I promise to go back to Hawaii with you if you'll just indulge me in this one thing. You both want to be sure Erik's okay, don't you? Ian, please," she pleaded when they hesitated.

Ian sighed.

"Well, what are we doing standing here? Let's go book our flight to Juneau."

"You're going with me?"

"All the way to Erik's cabin if necessary."

Her lips curved in a smile before she rushed forward and hugged them both.

"Thank you."

"Just be sure you stand up for us when we have to face our wives," Caleb muttered.

"Works both ways. I'm probably going to need your help explaining this to Erik."

Ian called Ernest to let him know their plans. Ernest offered to send a man named Burt to the airport and take them directly to the cabin. They spotted Burt holding a sign when they arrived. Ernest gave Ian a few details to be sure they didn't somehow get tricked by Wayne and go

148

with the wrong man. Burt looked very professional dressed in the dark suit of a chauffeur.

"There he is," Ian said, taking Riley by the elbow and urging her forward.

"Are you sure? How do you know he's the right guy?"

"See the sign he's holding?"

She nodded.

"JD. What's that supposed to stand for?"

"Short for John Doe. That's what Ernest told me to watch for. I have a few key words to exchange with him that Ernest also suggested. Come on, let's see if we're on the same script."

The three of them walked up to Burt and stopped. He held the sign steady and his expression didn't waver. "I heard the fishing is pretty good here this time of year," Ian said.

"The fishing is always good in Alaska," Burt replied, shaking Ian's hand.

Riley laughed. "Those are your key words?"

"Who cares as long as we get out of here before Wackco Wayne shows up," Caleb grunted.

They followed Burt outside.

"The car's this way."

"Did Ernest send a limousine? I've only ridden in one once, but I enjoyed it," Riley said.

"Then you're going to love my Jeep."

Consciousness returned via waves of pain radiating throughout Erik's body. His eyelids dragged open drawing attention to the throbbing inside his head. Pulsing needles tingled along his bound wrists and ankles. Muscles protested the hard surface where he lay cramped and stiff. He took in shaky breaths trying to orient himself to what brought him to this state. Facts slowly began to filter through his bruised brain.

Saving Arthur from committing suicide. The long drive to the cabin and opening the door finding his father gagged and bound to a chair looking wild eyed with terror. Focusing on freeing Edward blocked out all other sights and sounds until the blow to the back of his head alerted Erik too late that his presence didn't bring the reaction he expected. He reeled like a man in a drunken stupor seconds before his knees buckled and he collapsed to the floor blacking out as he fell.

Was his father all right? Who was their assailant? Where was Arthur? He gritted his teeth against the pain, as he twisted his body into position until he could locate his father. Edward sat unmoving now still bound, but with his head hanging forward as a large circle of blood stained the front of his shirt. Erik spotted Arthur sitting at the table staring at him.

"Arthur, for the love of God, don't just sit there! Help my dad."

"Why would I do that when I was the one who shot him?"

What madness was this? "I was under the impression you came here to shoot yourself."

"That is still part of the plan. I want you to understand I killed your father because he deserved to die. You know the old saying, 'an eye for an eye'."

"Are you implying you murdered my Dad in retaliation for something he did to you?"

Arthur stared at Edward. "He caused my granddaughter to end her own life. Chelsey was the only family I had and it's Edward's fault that I've lost her."

"I'm truly sorry about your granddaughter. I came here as soon as I heard about her death, but I didn't know my father was involved. I came because I wanted to help you."

Tears flooded Arthur's eyes streaming down wrinkled cheeks. "It's too late for that now."

"What did my dad have to do with Chelsey's death? I'm at a loss to understand this."

"She was such a lovely girl with the prettiest blue eyes that just made you want to melt. She was a sweet girl, but too naïve for her own good. Edward took advantage of her inexperience with men and lured her into having an affair with him."

"I never heard anything about that," Erik said, trying to understand where this conversation was going to end up leading him considering he was dealing with a man consumed with grief.

"No one knew. Your father made sure the affair was kept a secret. He told Chelsey it would ruin his reputation, which isn't too surprising knowing Edward King only cared about himself. She actually thought he loved her and would one day ask her to marry him."

"Poor Chelsey. No wonder you hate my father."

"I went to Edward when I found out about the affair and demanded he leave her alone. He told me to mind my own business and threatened to cook up some story about me stealing from the company if I tried to interfere. I went to Chelsey and begged her to break it off with him."

"But she didn't, I take it."

Arthur's facial muscles twisted. "No, but Edward did when she told him she was pregnant."

"Jesus. What did my dad do then?" But Erik had a feeling he already knew his father wouldn't have done anything to stand by the girl.

"He accused her of sleeping around and told her to get an abortion. She refused and he threw her away as though she was nothing more than a piece of garbage. That's why I had to kill him."

"I understand your motive, but you must know you will go to prison. You'll need a good lawyer. Let me help you."

Arthur patted the rifle lying across his knees. "I won't be needing a lawyer because I'm going to be taking care of myself. But thank you for offering. You've always been a good boy, Erik. It's nice to know you didn't inherit your father's rotten genes. I have nothing against you, but I would like to get it off my chest that I did try to kill you once."

Stunned, Erik gawked at him. "You were responsible for my plane going down?"

"Yes. I went to Juneau and fooled with the engine. I used to be a bush pilot, so I knew how."

"I thought you said you didn't have anything against me."

"I did it because I thought Edward's grief would make him give up Chelsey, but he didn't care. You are well rid of him because he hated that you were everything Ernest wanted in a son."

An unfamiliar ache settled in Erik's chest.

"I knew he wasn't very fond of me, but I didn't realize he actually hated me."

"He did. He sat there and blubbered like a coward telling me to kill you and spare him."

"You got your revenge, and you don't have a beef with me. So, how about untying me?"

"I can't."

"Why not?"

"Because I made a promise to someone to keep you here."

"Damn." A trap had been set, and Erik had walked right into it with eyes wide open.

The dryness in his throat made it difficult to swallow, and his insides felt like he was being eaten up by nerves. He wasn't one hundred per cent happy with the full logistics of his plan, but if things worked out the way he hoped, Wayne believed he would be able to get his life back on his terms. He'd had enough of the financial and emotional blackmail he'd been forced to endure.

All he needed was enough luck to have each part of his plan fall into place. Then, he could be his own man again.

Of course, it was going to take more than luck for everything to go the way it must. He took a chance that Riley would fall for his story about the danger of Erik having a flashback. Thank God she went for it. He must be a better actor than he thought. Good thing because he already called Richard to tell him why Riley went to Miami. He knew Richard didn't like anyone pulling a fast one on him, especially a woman. Wayne relied on that particular phobia and laid it on real thick about how Riley laughed that she got away with her scheme.

He explained how she and Erik worked together to trick Richard. Wayne also made sure Richard knew it was Erik's influence on Riley that was keeping her money out of his hands. He had to be sure Richard understood he would have paid his share if only Erik didn't have that kind of influence over Riley.

Richard became as furious as Wayne hoped he would and for once he didn't mind hearing the man's terrible temper tantrum, since it wasn't directed at him personally. Wayne explained if Richard came to Alaska, he would be able to get his revenge on both Erik and Riley at a remote cabin. He would be able to do anything he wanted without fear of being discovered.

Wayne almost felt sorry for Erik and Riley thinking about the terrible things Richard would probably do to them before he ended their lives. But he forced that sympathy away. Why should he feel any pity for them when they'd brought their own fate on themselves? He wasn't the one who asked Riley to go to Miami and confront Richard, and Erik wouldn't be breathing down his neck if she hadn't gone poking around where she had no business looking.

Wayne went back to focusing on his plan. The hard part was going to be stalling Riley until Richard could arrive. It helped he would be able to close that time gap somewhat with her having a layover in Seattle. He rubbed his forehead, searching his brain as he tried to come up with an excuse to keep Riley from being suspicious when he didn't drive her to the cabin right away.

Getting to Erik as quickly as possible was the ploy he'd used to convince Riley to leave Hawaii so she wasn't going to be content with waiting. He already made his arrangements for Richard to meet him at the airport, but to keep out of sight until Riley was in the car. Wayne knew it would be best to allow Richard to restrain her in whatever way he chose.

Once again, a pang of remorse for what Riley was probably going to have to endure nibbled at the edges of Wayne's conscience, but not enough to stop him. No, not nearly enough. He even managed to smile. It felt good knowing he would soon be rid of his antagonists. He'd been stomped on long enough. Now his chance to do his own crushing was about to happen.

Richard would take care of Erik and Riley and he would personally take care of Richard. It was going to feel so good watching that murdering blackmailer die.

The beauty of it all was that he would use Arthur as his scapegoat by telling the authorities the old man had flipped out.

Arthur had probably already gotten rid of Edward King, an annoying human if there ever was one. He just happened to be standing outside of Edward's office the day Arthur went there ranting and raving about Edward's affair with Arthur's granddaughter.

Another great thing about all this plotting was going to finally be the key to him having his chance to head up ELK. It was a job Wayne expected to have when Edward bombed, and Erik became a hermit. It'd been humiliating when Ernest put Frances at the helm instead, especially when she made it quite clear she didn't want the responsibility. Wayne knew very well that old buzzard deliberately overlooked him on purpose.

Well, Ernest wasn't going to have much choice when he looked around and Wayne was the only obvious one to run things now. Options were limited when you insisted on keeping a business in the family. He wasn't a blood relative and Ernest never let him forget that. But Frances would surely stand by him if she no longer had her brother.

In fact, he was counting on her full support and it was about time she came around.

Wayne wasn't looking forward to having to deal with her reaction when Erik turned up dead. It wasn't going to be pretty. On the other hand, this could force her to give him the respect he deserved not only in the business, but also as a husband and father. And if he was honest, Wayne realized he did care more about having that respect via running ELK than he did for any mushy family bonding. It was past time Frances accepted the reality of their relationship.

THE LONELY ONES
Olivia Claire High

Wayne closed his eyes for a few moments picturing himself finally sitting behind Ernest's big desk, issuing orders, and having people bow down to him for a change. What a great vision. Yes sirree. No more feeling like secondhand goods. He would be the head guy.

And to think all this was going to be made possible thanks to one man. He had a lot to thank Arthur for. Too bad the old fellow wasn't going to be around to share in the wealth. But the man didn't want to live anyway, now that he lost his granddaughter.

Arthur was probably thanking him right now for helping him get his revenge. Revenge. Wayne liked the sound of that. His brain was finally winning over the brawn of the King family. He was showing them you could have strength, but still be weak. He liked the idea of that a lot.

But most of all, he wondered how Erik liked being made to grovel for a change.

Chapter Sixteen

Erik felt like an idiot knowing now how easily Wayne had fooled him into coming here. He couldn't decide if he was angry or just plain frustrated with himself for falling for Wayne's lies. Both, he supposed considering he hadn't been able to convince Arthur to untie him, let alone to let him go.

"No need for inuendoes. I know you're talking about Wayne. He and I weren't exactly best buddies, but I didn't know he hated me, too. Nice to find out both my father and my brother-in-law held me in such high esteem."

"Don't be bitter about that. Your father could never care about anyone but himself. The man was born flawed and that made it impossible for him to understand what it meant to love anyone, even his own children. You really are better off having him be dead."

"Not like this, Arthur. Not just for the pleasure of killing. What about Wayne? What does he hope to gain by all this?"

"Power."

"I thought he just wanted to be head bookkeeper."

"He wants it all; and with you out of the way he can head up ELK. It's all he's ever wanted."

Erik snorted.

"He'll run the company into the ground faster than my father did, considering the way Wayne handles the books. I should have paid more attention when I came back. Then I would have discovered all the money he was pulling out for my dad's gambling."

"Is that what he told you?" Arthur chuckled. "That boy sure knows how to spin a tale. No one studied your father as much as I have trying to find his weaknesses, and I can tell you gambling wasn't one of them."

"What about Dad's trips to Las Vegas?" Erik asked, confused.

"He went a couple of times, is all."

"Well, one would have been all it took to meet Richard Melvin and have him show up the day of the rafting accident."

"Richard Melvin, the one who sued ELK?"

"That's right."

Arthur shook his head.

"More of the tale. Your father never even heard about that man until the lawsuit. I'm sure Richard Melvin ended up coming to Juneau because he sent himself."

"I recently have reason to believe he came to kill his wife."

"I wouldn't be surprised. Her falling out of the raft sounded kind of odd to me at the time."

"Did you know Melvin has been blackmailing Wayne ever since that day because he took a photo of Wayne tampering with my vest?"

"You don't say? No, I didn't know that, but now it makes sense why Wayne messed around with his bookkeeping to get money."

"But you obviously know enough about my brother-in-law to understand what kind of a person he is. Doesn't it bother you that he's coming here to kill me? After all, he can't afford to let me live now that I know so much. You already killed my father. Isn't that enough? You got what you wanted. Could you at least put a blanket over Dad's body?"

"No. I waited a long time to get even, and I like looking at him like this," he said in a hollow voice devoid of emotion.

Erik worried Arthur had lost touch with realty from being mired in the grief of losing his granddaughter. He talked as though he'd promised Wayne to pay him back for a favor, rather than convincing him to set a man up to be murdered. Wayne must be gloating right now.

"You and I don't have a quarrel with each other. You helped me build this cabin. You stayed here and went hunting with me when I was really messed up. I need your help now. Wayne is going to come for me. Cut me loose, so I can at least defend myself."

"I don't know. My word is my bond and I did promise Wayne, like I said."

"Was your word your bond when you promised to help me when we built this place?"

"You know it was."

"Then what's changed between us now? We've been good friends for a long time, Arthur. You know that. Wayne told me you came here to commit suicide. I believed him enough to want to prevent that. I came here in good faith. Is this your way of thanking me?"

Arthur rubbed a hand down his face.

"I don't know what to do. You're confusing me."

"You killed my dad. You got your revenge. Don't make Wayne turn you into the kind of man he is. He's a coward and a cheat without any sense of decency or loyalty. You didn't let my father get away with that behavior, so why are you giving in to Wayne. Cut me loose, Arthur."

"I got to think about this."

The longer he stayed, the more difficult it became for Erik to block out the stench of his father's blood and seeing his lifeless body. He needed to get his own body working again.

"Could we go outside while you do your thinking?"

"I guess we could. I need to use the privy anyway."

"I do, too. I hope you will untie me for that."

"I'm only going to untie you just enough to do what you have to do, but don't forget my gun will still be aimed at you."

Erik hoped he'd be able to break free. He knew it wasn't going to be easy. His muscles were cramped from being bound for so long. He decided to continue to try and get some type of advantage by appealing to Arthur's conscience. The only thing he really had going for him was their years of friendship, but that was proving to be a bit shaky right now.

"We both know Wayne is a coward, but I never thought of you as being one, too."

"I am not a coward!" he yelled, bringing some color back into his cheeks.

"The Arthur I've known would never hold an innocent man captive. Nor would he be pointing a gun at an unarmed man. You gave me a lot of good advice over the years and one of the most important things you said was to not take advantage of a man when he was down."

Arthur slumped back against the chair, his earlier outburst waning.

"I'm not the man I used to be. Your father's wickedness changed all that. He turned me into someone I never thought I would be. I'm sorry."

"Then don't be like him because if you do that means he got the best of you in the end."

"I don't know what to do anymore."

Erik pressed on when he realized Arthur might finally be faltering.

"Be the good man you've always been."

Arthur's hands tightened on his rifle.

"I can't."

"Not even for Chelsey?"

Riley sat in the front seat next to Burt and stared through the windshield while he drove around trees. She never let her eyes leave the winding pathway that seemed to exist only in Burt's mind. Ian and Caleb sat in the back doing their own surveying, studying the landscape.

"Are you sure you know where you're going?" Riley asked. "There isn't any defined route."

"Not to mention the trees are all beginning to look a lot alike," Caleb observed.

"I've driven this way many times before."

Riley shot him a quick glance before staring straight ahead again.

"You have? How come?"

"You don't think Ernest King would let his grandson be out here all alone months at a time without anyone checking on him, do you?"

"Erik never mentioned anything about you coming to see him."

"He didn't know. I always parked out of sight and was very careful to make sure he wouldn't see me."

"I'm really glad to know that. I remember telling Erik I thought it was risky living out here without any contact from the outside world."

"That was how he wanted things."

Burt pulled into a small grove of trees and shut off the engine.

"This is where I used to park to keep hidden from Erik. We have to hoof it from it, but the cabin isn't far."

They climbed out of the Jeep and at a nod from Burt began to follow him in single file. They trudged on in silence, eyes darting around them until he stopped behind a line of trees where they could see the cabin. Ian and Caleb looked at each other. Ian put his hand on Riley's shoulder.

"It would be best if you stayed here until we can check things out."

"I agree," Burt said.

"What? No! I didn't come all this way not to see Erik. I want to go with you."

"You will, but just not right now," Caleb said.

"This Arthur supposedly came here to kill himself. We don't know what we're going to find. Let us make sure what's happened and then one of us will come and get you."

"But . . ."

"No buts, Riley."

She knew when Caleb used that tone of voice, he would end up tying her to a tree to keep her here if she continued to argue with him. Not only that, she was up against three very determined looking men. She shoved her hands into the pockets of her jeans and stepped back.

"Fine, but I'm going to be worrying myself to death if you take too long. Please hurry."

"We will," Ian assured her, giving her shoulder a reassuring squeeze.

Burt waved them forward but held his hand up seconds later when the sound of a vehicle approaching broke the silence. They dashed behind separate trees, each tightening their bodies trying to make themselves as small as possible. Every pair of eyes watched with tense interest as a dark blue SUV pulled up in front of the cabin and stopped.

Burt mouthed, "Wayne."

The group waited and observed from their individual vantagepoints. Riley managed to hold her breath when

Wayne emerged, but she couldn't contain a gasp when another man opened the passenger door and stepped out. She motioned to Caleb, behind a nearby tree. He ran over to her.

"Th . . . that's Richard Melvin," she told him in a stammering whisper.

"Damn! That can't be good," Caleb mumbled and zipped the short distance over to Burt.

Burt's mouth thinned into a tight line.

"He's probably armed, if he's as bad as I've heard. You better come back to the Jeep with me and get the guns Ernest sent. He told me you know how to handle them."

"Guns?" Riley said, her mouth gaping open.

"Why did Ernest think you'd need to be armed? Did he know Richard was going to be here?"

"No, but he didn't want to take any chances. What's to keep this guy from taking Arthur's gun? Come on," he said, waving to the others and they took off running to the Jeep.

Burt handed Ian and Caleb their weapons with a warning that they didn't try to be heroes. Burt suggested Riley stay with him now. But once again she begged to not be left behind. They agreed only after she promised to stay at a certain spot until they came for her, as planned before. Burt opted to remain with the Jeep if they ended up having to make a quick exit.

They went their separate ways, each preparing themselves for whatever awaited them.

Erik sat on a fallen log while Arthur took a stump for his seat. The fresh air afforded a welcome relief from the stench of death. But the throbbing in Erik's head still pounded like a fist against his temples while his arms and legs burned with the pain of blood rushing through them.

Erik's talking had done little good in convincing Arthur to free him. Every time he thought the old man was on the verge of weakening enough to put down his rifle, he would go back to insisting he promised to hold Erik for Wayne.

Erik tried to think of another tactic when the sound of footsteps crunching over the hard ground broke into his thoughts. Both he and Arthur looked up seconds before Wayne came running into the clearing followed by Richard Melvin. Both men banished their guns before Richard turned his gun on Arthur.

The shot sent Arthur to his knees. Erik instinctively rolled off his log where he flopped on the ground trying to shield himself while bullets went flying. He peered over the edge just in time to see Arthur fire a fatal shot back at Richard. Wayne stood looking from one to the other in a daze at the grim scene before him seconds before he recovered enough to fire his gun at Erik.

The bullet hit the log sending a chip of wood against Erik's face slicing open a gash against one cheek. Erik flinched as pain tore into flesh. He knew Wayne was a lousy shot, and this time he was grateful for that lack of skill. But luck wasn't with him when Wayne started walking toward the log. Even a lousy marksman wouldn't be able to miss such an easy target.

Erik inhaled what he believed would be his last breath when voices coming from inside the cabin carried outside.

Wayne abandoned Erik and took off running around one side of the building, just as Ian and Caleb appeared in the clearing. Ian hurried over to Erik while Caleb bent down to check the two men on the ground.

"They're both dead," he said and rushed over to where Ian was pressing a handkerchief over Erik's wounded cheek.

"We need to get you out of these ropes."

"Check Arthur's pockets for a knife. I'm okay, but one of you should go after my brother-in-law. I don't want that little worm getting away."

Riley would be flying if she had wings, the way she ran toward the cabin when she heard guns being fired. She headed straight for the cabin when Wayne rammed right into her. His shock lasted mere seconds before he grabbed her by the arm and pulled her toward his car.

"Let me go!" she yelled, digging at his fingers trying to free herself.

"Listen to me. We have to leave before Richard discovers I slipped away and comes gunning for us!" He shoved her into his car and shot out two tires on each of the vehicles.

"What are you doing? You can't leave Erik without a way to escape?" Riley screamed.

"I don't want Richard having a way to follow us. He forced me to drive him here. He's on a rampage looking for you."

"What about Erik and my friends? We can't just leave them."

"Your friends are armed and can take care of themselves. They would want me to keep you safe. They can catch up with us later. Now stop talking and drive, for God's sake."

Riley started the engine and began to steer the car away from the cabin. "I don't think I can find my way back to the road." Wayne looked around, as she drove. "How did you get here?"

"Ernest hired a man to bring us. He's waiting just up ahead by his Jeep. There."

Wayne saw where she pointed and shot out two tires sending Burt scrambling for cover.

"Are you out of your mind? Now you've really left Erik with no way out of here."

"It would also be transport for Richard. Keep going. I want to be well away from here. We will call for help as soon as we can get a phone signal."

Riley gripped the wheel.

"Tell me if you were able to see Erik."

"I saw him."

"Is he all right?"

"I think we should talk about that later."

"Not later, now!"

"Don't say I didn't try to spare you, but there's one less male member of the King family."

A cry slipped from Riley's lips, as she stomped on the brake. Not only has she lost the man she loved, but now she had also put Ian and Caleb in danger. Would they be killed, too? She pressed her hands to her face while her body shook with hysterical sobbing.

Wayne shook her by the shoulder and spoke in a sharp tone.

"I know you are upset, but we have to save our grieving for later. We need to get help."

Riley gulped back a sob, white knuckling the steering wheel. "How did you get away?"

"I ran into the cabin through the backdoor when Richard wasn't looking."

Riley's eyes darkened with suspicion.

"You're lying. I happen to know there isn't any backdoor in the cabin."

Wayne blinked in surprise and shrugged.

"Well, it looks like you caught me. A man is bound to slip up I suppose, when he has so many details to keep in his head."

"Did you kill Erik?"

"No. I didn't have to and now that we have that detail out of the way you will start driving again. I told you I want to get out of here."

"Oh, I'll drive, but we're going back to the cabin, so I can find out what really happened."

"You are not going back to the cabin," Wayne contradicted in an icy voice. "I'm telling you what to do, not the other way around." He raised his gun and aimed it at her temple making Riley cower back in fear. "I advise you to do as I say because I've dreamed of getting even with you for what you've done to screw up my life. Makes me happy just thinking it."

His grin reminded Riley of an evil gargoyle. She had little doubt he intended to kill her but seemed to be saving her demise for later. Perhaps he needed her as a hostage for a while. He waved the gun near her face.

"What's it to be? Die now or drive?"

She drove.

Chapter Seventeen

"I thought you wanted to help Erik."

He snarled out a string of cuss words. "I may have had to tolerate him, but I most certainly never wanted to help him. Anyway, I don't have to be concerned about him anymore."

"Stop saying that!"

"Why? Is the truth too much for your sensitive ears? You only have yourself to blame for all this, you know. Everything was going along okay until you stuck your nose into my business."

"What did you have against Erik? He's treated you fairly."

Wayne pulled the gun back away from Riley's head, but kept it pointed at her with a steady hand. He let out a derisive snort.

"Fairly? You call it *fair* when I'm being made to walk in his shadow and work my ass off for the King family, only to have them give all the perks to their favorite son? I'm the one who helped Frances hold things together when Erik ran off and dumped everything in her lap. Did he get punished for that? Ernest wouldn't think of blaming his perfect grandson. I should have slipped a mickey in that old man's cognac years ago."

"Why didn't you just tell them how you felt, instead of . . . of sending Erik to die?" Riley stammered, her lips trembling.

"What you don't know about Ernest is a lot. I knew the moment Frances introduced us he wasn't going to accept me. I could see he despised me from the first. I may have married into the family, but I could never be one of them. Arthur saved me the trouble of killing Erik myself."

"Arthur? You said he went to the cabin to kill himself."

"I said a lot of things. I had to come up with something to get you to come here and Erik to go to the cabin. Luckily, I remembered old Art had his own issues with the Kings."

"What issues?"

"There you go being nosy again. Don't you ever learn? You should be asking yourself if it was worth snooping to the point that you caused Richard to come here looking for you after you played him for a sucker. He was very unhappy about that and when Richard is unhappy someone is bound to suffer. But it won't be me this time. Let everyone have their shoot-out at the cabin and save me from having to dirty my hands. Oh, and you should know Richard brought someone with him to wait at your apartment to finish you off if he doesn't get a chance to do it himself."

A deep sense of dread made Riley's hands shake on the wheel as she thought about Richard's dead wives. "I just wanted to help Erik find out the truth about Mrs. Melvin's death."

"You've said that before and look where your so-called help has gotten you. But since you are so set on fixing everyone else's problems, you can help me get away. I'm going to need funds, which you will provide from your own money."

"Over my dead body," she blurted before she could stop herself.

"That can be arranged, but it will be an accident. You should be glad it'll be me and not Richard. I doubt if he would make your demise as quick as I will, given how much he wants to show you just what he does to people who make a fool of him. But that's his problem."

Beads of sweat trickled between Riley's breasts hearing Wayne talk about her death like it was a minor detail he would cross off a list of chores he needed to complete.

"It boggles my mind to think how you will be able to explain all of this to Frances, especially about Erik."

"I'm not going to waste my breath explaining anything to her. Ernest has probably filled her mind with poison against me by now. It's out of my hands. Richard left instructions to go after the family. Part of the deal I made with him was to call her and say it was safe to come home."

Riley's foot slipped on the accelerator making the car wobble going over a particularly rough spot on the ground. "In the name of God, this is your wife and children you are sacrificing. Surely you don't want anything to happen to them."

"Don't I? She never went out of her way to defend me against all the insults I've had to put up with. As to the boys, I never wanted those brats. She stopped using birth control without telling me, so she could get pregnant. Whatever happens to them will be on her head."

"You are despicable beyond words," Riley hissed out with contempt, not caring if she angered him. "How can you be so coldhearted when Frances married you in good faith?"

"She's also a King first and foremost. You think I don't know she's always compared me to her precious brother and I'm the one who ends up coming up short? Well, no more. I've lived my life the way her family wanted me to long enough. Now I'm going to live my life my way."

"Not if you're in prison."

"They will have to catch me first. You and your money will be my ticket out of here. I hoped to head up ELK once Erik was gone, but now I can see it will be best for me to leave Alaska. I'm sure I'll find someplace that will suit me nicely. I rather fancy a life living abroad."

Rebellion boiled inside Riley. Wayne took her man from her and now he wanted her money to help him escape before he ended her life, too. He didn't care who had to die to get his own way, even if his insidious plan meant sacrificing his wife and children. A red haze filled Riley's vision. She thought Richard Melvin was a murdering psychopath. But Wayne was turning out to be much worse by pretending he ever cared about the wellbeing of anyone other than himself.

Erik would have done everything in his power to protect Frances and the boys. But Erik wasn't here. Pain stabbed her in the chest knowing she hadn't been able to save him, but she refused to allow Wayne to continue with his evil plans to harm Frances and the children. They were innocent victims coming home to be slaughtered.

Riley understood she was perilously close to dying herself.

But she wasn't dead yet.

Back at the cabin, Erik stared at Ian his mouth gone slack with stunned disbelief.

"What do you mean Wayne has Riley? What was she doing here?"

"Trying to save you," Ian said and explained Wayne's ruse to lure her here.

"Damn him to hell! Go after her. I'll catch up, but I have to do something in the cabin first."

Caleb cleared his throat.

"I don't think you should go in there right now. There's, um . . ."

"A dead man. I know. It's my father. Arthur killed him."

Ian and Caleb both raised their eyebrows. "Jesus," they muttered together.

Caleb recovered first.

"I'm sorry, Erik. I know what it's like to lose a father. Not in the same way as you have, but mine's gone nevertheless."

"Then you know there's a point where you can't do anything to bring them back. I'm more concerned about Riley right now. Please go after her."

"We can't. That's another glitch. Wayne shot out a couple tires on all the vehicles, including Burt's Jeep. I just got back from talking to him," Caleb continued. He's already heading to the nearest main road to try and flag someone down, or at least be able to get a signal on his phone. He's not sure when he'll be able to get back, so he suggested we put Melvin's and Arthur's bodies in the cab of the old man's truck because the scent of blood could draw predators."

"He's right, but I'd still like you to go after Riley, as soon as we take care of the bodies. Wayne already has a big head start." Erik stared at the cabin. "I don't think I'll ever be able to come back here again."

"Why would you want to? It reminds me of a morgue. Do you need help inside?" Ian asked.

"Thanks, but I need to do this on my own. I'm about to say goodbye to a man who never even wanted me to say hello." His bland expression did little to disguise the edginess in his voice and the haunted look in his eyes.

"Just find Riley." He wiped a hand down his face smearing blood from the wound on his cheek. "She's all that matters now."

Riley pressed two shaky fingers against Wayne's throat and jerked her hand away. She hadn't meant for him to die when she veered the car into a tree. She only wanted to divert his attention away from her long enough so she could get out of the car and try to outrun him. How ironic! His death was caused by something that was supposed to save him. The impact from the inflating air bag made Wayne's finger accidently press the trigger causing him to shoot himself.

She had her own problems when the air bag on her side kept her pinned until she finally managed to wriggle out from under it. Her entire upper body hurt from being slammed back against the seat creating the sensation that an anvil was sitting on her chest, her neck was caught in a vise, and a hammer was pounding inside her head.

Pain and the ordeal of having a gun pointed at her made her stomach cramp with nausea. Her headache didn't help when she tried to concentrate. But she had enough wits to know there were dead men back at the cabin and a dead man in this car. No one would mind if Richard wouldn't be around to plague people ever again. What about Arthur?

But the most heart wrenching loss was knowing she hadn't saved Erik. How had everything gone so wrong when all she wanted to do was make things right? Who would want her when she had proven herself to be a magnet for trouble? She took one last look at Wayne's dead body and fought to breathe, as she rubbed her sore chest. Wayne was beyond help and perhaps she was, too unless she could somehow do something that would bring a modicum of restitution to the people who she had harmed the most.

Riley staggered out of the woods and accepted a ride with a young couple who drove her to town. She borrowed the girl's coat to cover her bloodied shirt after explaining she ran her car into a tree. Riley's one driving need was to warn Frances about Richard's intention to harm her and the boys. She debated how she would explain Wayne and Erik's deaths. She ended up playing the coward by sending a text. Frances would find out the gruesome details soon enough.

Riley had the teenagers drive her to the bank where she withdrew all her money from her savings account making the teller's eyes widen. She would be using cash from now on because credit cards left a paper trail making it too easy to find a person and she did not want to be found. She paid the girl to buy her a new set of clothes, had them drive her to a ferry, and gave them a generous tip for their help.

The ferry ended up being the first leg of a long journey, as she headed south without any idea where she would end up. Riley knew she began a new chapter in her life when she left her home in Hawaii to come to Alaska. She remembered being filled with excited anticipation at the thought of making a fresh start. There were some down times but falling in love and being with Erik had made her life so right.

How could she know that everything would end up going so terribly wrong?

Keeping track of time wasn't a priority when you didn't care what day it was. Riley bought a few more clothes and some toiletries along the way before continuing a trip that didn't have a destination. She finally ran out of energy after traveling over sixteen hundred miles and ending up in the town of Blaine, Washington. She decided to stay . . . at least until she could begin to form a more rational plan for her future.

A future she didn't much care about at this point in her life.

Blaine was a city within the metropolitan area of Bellingham with a population of just under five thousand. The city's northern boundary was the Canada-U.S. border. Riley stayed at a local motel for the first few nights until she realized she wanted a more comfortable lodging.

She rented a little four room cottage. The place was fully furnished, which saved her having to spend time and money buying anything to make the place livable. It also helped that she immediately liked the owners, Jed and Sally White. She didn't know how to answer when they asked how long she would be needing the cottage and felt grateful when they didn't press her.

Riley did explain she had just lost someone very dear to her and wanted time alone to heal. They expressed concern for her wellbeing and made it clear she only had to call if she needed anything. Their understanding and kindness brought tears to Riley's eyes. She discovered crying had become something she did far too often, especially when she thought about Erik.

Riley found herself often dreaming they would go someplace together and always end up getting separated. She'd search and search, but she could never find him. She awoke feeling heartbroken all over again. She also had another frequent dream that was even more of a nightmare. Always the same and always just as frightening. People who looked like Richard Melvin surrounded her. Riley would run until she came to a forest hoping to hide, but her tormentors appeared from behind every tree.

A car would come, but not to rescue her. She recognized Wayne driving, despite the blood covering most of his face. His demonic expression caused her heart to pound so hard it felt as though the organ would erupt right out of her chest. She couldn't outrun him no matter how hard she tried. By the time she awoke with a scream ripping from her throat, she had taken his place behind the wheel with hands covered in blood while he stared at her with dead, accusing eyes.

Riley couldn't shake the horror, or the sense that she might end up dying one of those nights. Most days she could barely get out of bed and when she did the hours stretched long and lonely in front of her. She stayed in the cottage day after day punishing herself by continuing to harbor regrets for the damage she'd inflicted on Erik and his family. She barely slept and had trouble choking down any food. She ate less and dreamed more as time went on until she began to resemble a walking corpse.

A pipe began leaking beneath the bathroom sink weeks after Riley moved into the cottage. She taped it, but the leak grew bad enough that she had to put a pan beneath to catch the water. The bathroom was close enough to the bedroom to make it impossible not to hear the dripping. Riley closed the bathroom door only to be greeted by the steady noise of water escaping.

She finally forced herself to call Jed when the monotonous dripping began to pound inside her head like the rushing waterfall making Riley cover her ears with two pillows. He came to do the repair. Riley invited him into the house but ended up going outside to the backyard when he became too chatty. She didn't mean to be rude. It was just that she couldn't find the energy to take part in a conversation. She went back into the house when Jed called to her the plumbing problem was fixed. Riley thanked him and remembered at the last minute to say hello to Sally.

Jed did more than that.

He told his wife when he got home how sickly Riley looked. A nurturing person like Sally could never allow someone to suffer without trying to do something to help. She packed a large basket, got into her car that same afternoon, and marched right passed a flabbergasted Riley straight into the kitchen where she started setting containers on the table.

Riley rubbed her forehead in confusion. "Um, what are you doing?"

"I brought you something to eat."

"That's very sweet of you, but I can get my own food."

Sally's eyes did a quick sweep of Riley's emaciated body. "I don't think you've been doing much of that. When's the last time you ate a decent meal?"

She continued to place the dishes on the table when Riley didn't respond. A bowl of homemade chicken soup, a slice of freshly baked bread smeared with jam, and a dish of fruit sat waiting when she finished. She pulled out a chair and pointed to the food.

"I'm not leaving here until you eat."

"I appreciate what you're doing, but I'm not really hungry right now. I promise to eat later."

"Would you rather I have Jed come and hold you down while I feed you myself?"

The look of determination on Sally's face and the way she crossed her arms over her ample breasts left little room for argument. Riley conceded defeat and sat. The sooner she ate, the sooner Sally might go, as uncharitable as that sounded.

"Eat the soup first while it's hot."

Riley took a taste. "It's delicious. Am I right in thinking this and the bread are homemade?"

"Yes, and the jam. I also brought my own blend of herbal tea. Will you join me in a cup?"

"Yes, I believe I will," Riley said, knowing it would probably be a waste of breath to refuse.

It took Riley a bit of effort to finish all the food considering how little she'd eaten lately.

"Thank you, Sally. I guess I needed someone to remind me I haven't been taking very good care of myself. I don't want you to think I'm ungrateful, but I . . ." her voice trailed off.

Sally reached across the table and gave Riley's hand a gentle pat. "You told us why you came here. I can see the grief has taken a toll on you. But sometimes it helps to talk to someone about your sorrows. I know each person's loss is unique to them and you think I wouldn't understand, but Jed and I know what it's like to lose a loved one, too."

"I'm sorry for your loss. Did it happen recently?"

"Thirty years ago, but it still feels like yesterday."

"I guess I've been so wrapped up in my own self-pity I forget I'm not the only one to suffer such terrible emptiness. May I ask what happened to you and Jed?"

Sally took a few moments before she spoke.

"It began the day I picked up our daughter after school when we were having some pretty heavy rain."

"You have a daughter?"

"Had."

Riley wanted to bite her tongue when she saw the anguish in Sally's eyes. "You don't have to tell me. Please forget I asked."

"Talking reminds me she really did exist. I took a different route home that day. A drunk driver lost control of his pickup and slammed into my car. He hit the passenger side. My Elaine died before anyone could get her out of the car. She was our only child and would have been ten in a couple of days. I had her gifts hidden in the closet and plans made for her birthday party."

Riley closed her eyes for several seconds picturing an excited little girl who would never open another gift, or see her mother bake her another birthday cake. She looked at Sally.

"Losing a child must be beyond painful. I hope the drunk driver was punished."

"Losing anyone you love is always painful. He did go to prison, but it couldn't bring my daughter back. I wanted to pick Elaine up at school because I thought it would be better for her given the weather. She would be alive today if I had let her take the bus like she usually did."

"I hope you aren't blaming yourself for her death. It clearly was the drunk driver's fault."

"I know, but I will always regret taking that different way home."

"Were you injured yourself?"

"Yes, and I have the scars. But it's the scars on the inside that bother me the most."

"I believe I understand what you mean."

Riley bit her lip.

"How did you learn to cope?"

"I didn't do very well for a long time until I finally realized I couldn't continue to bury myself under the weight of grief knowing how much Jed needed me. He was grieving, too. It helps to tell myself Elaine is still with us," Sally explained and touched a hand over her heart.

"That's a beautiful way to think of her. You and Jed are so strong. I envy that."

"Your wounds are a lot fresher than mind. Do you feel like sharing what happened?"

Riley stared out the kitchen window. Two squirrels were scampering across the patch of lawn. What would it be like to be so carefree again? The only running she ever did these days was in her nightmares. Sally broke into her musing.

"It's okay if you'd rather not tell me. I only came to feed your body, not drain your soul."

"I have no soul. I gave it up the day I lost the man I wanted to marry. His name was Erik."

"Oh, my dear. Was he ill? Or did he perish in an accident?"

Riley took a sip of tea and set her cup back on the saucer.

"I murdered him."

Chapter Eighteen

Sally's cup rattled on her saucer. "I . . . I beg your pardon. Did you say you murdered him?"

"Yes. He was shot. I didn't physically pull the trigger, but I was the one responsible for putting him in danger. To make matters worse, he wasn't the only one to die because of me."

Riley told Sally what happened starting with the river incident, how her research led to Wayne's and Richard's crimes, and her leaving Alaska hoping to keep Frances and the boys safe.

Sally clutched a hand to her chest.

"My goodness! What a saga. I don't believe I've ever heard anything like it for real. No wonder you've been going through such a difficult time."

"Now you know why I came here and why I can never go back to my life in Juneau."

"Sometimes you have to go back before you can go forward again. It may help if you give yourself the opportunity to express regret to the family."

"I doubt it they would want to see me considering they know my part in all this."

"Have you been in contact with any of these people since you left?"

Riley took a sip of tea and mumbled,

"No."

"Then how do you know what they feel about you at this point in time? Sometimes people have to do their own forgiving in order to help themselves heal."

"Were you able forgive the man who killed Elaine?"

Sally nodded.

"Yes. Eventually. It was the only way I could go on living."

"That is so admirable of you, but what if I can't get forgiveness from the people I hurt?"

"Then you must learn to forgive yourself."

Riley thought Sally returned to check on her when the doorbell rang later that afternoon. But when she opened the door and saw the person who stood there her skin prickled with tiny jolts of electricity. A shocked squeak slipped between her quivering lips, her legs turned to jelly, and her body floated downward before being caught in her visitor's arms.

She awoke lying on the sofa and raised her eyelids slowly to focus on the man sitting by her.

"Deep breaths. You know, that's the second time you've fainted since we met. I'm going to have a complex if you keep doing that," Erik said, using humor to disguise his concern.

"What are you doing here?"

"Again, not the welcome I hoped for. Did you really think I wouldn't come for you?"

Riley rubbed her eyes, hard.

"Not if you're dead. This is just another dream and you'll be gone like always. I'm too tired to keep chasing after you. I can never catch you anyway. Go haunt someone else."

"Last time I checked I was very much alive."

"Either I'm going crazy, or this is some kind of sick joke."

"Neither one." His mouth slanted into a smile. "Why don't you try door number three?"

"I was told you died. That was awful enough, but it's not the only reason I left."

"I know. Frances told me about your message."

"Then you must know she has to hate me for what happened to Wayne."

"How can she hate a person who helped her face the truth?"

Erik put his arm around Riley when she struggled to sit up.

"The truth about what?"

"About who he really was behind his mask. Wayne's life was built on secrets and lies. He did a fair job hiding how he stole money from the company, but Fran realized he did an even better job making her believe he ever really cared about her and the boys."

"He certainly seemed concerned about her that day in your office."

"A smokescreen. He acted like he wanted to protect her when he really was only looking after his own skin. You gave him an unexpected wakeup call when you found the information about the offshore account. The only defense Wayne had was to turn on you and try to make Fran believe you were trying to victimize them."

Riley clasped and unclasped her hands.

"I didn't want to mention it to Frances in my message and I wouldn't be telling you if you hadn't already told me how things are back home. Wayne didn't care if Frances and the boys were murdered. It still makes me ill to think about it."

Fury flashed in Erik's eyes. "Like I said, he was only concerned about himself." He pulled an envelope out of his coat pocket and handed it to Riley. "She wrote you a letter explaining how she feels and that she doesn't blame you for any of what happened."

Riley took the envelope, stared at her name written on the front in Frances's neat hand, and set it aside.

"I appreciate that, but I'm sure they loved each other once. Maybe they would have worked things out if it hadn't been for me forcing Wayne into a corner."

"Frances doesn't believe they would. It wasn't just him stealing from ELK. Wayne had plans long before you came into the picture, and those plans included using the family to get what he wanted, but nothing to do with love or commitment to Fran and the kids. It was a lot easier for her to tell the boys their father died in an automobile accident than the truth."

"I want you to know I didn't shoot him. I made the car crash into a tree because he was pointing his gun at my head. It was all I could think to do to try and save myself. The gun went off when the air bag hit him. I didn't mean for him to die. I tried to help him, but it was too late."

Pity for her filled his eyes.

"He didn't deserve help. I'm sorry he put you through so much. It explains a lot about the trauma you've been dealing with because of how unhinged he became."

"The worse part was believing you were dead. Wayne said there was one less male member of the King family when I asked him if he saw you. I guess he lied to hurt me even more."

"He didn't lie about there being one less male King. He let you believe it was me, but he really meant my father."

"Your father?" Riley gripped the arm of the sofa. "Your father is dead?"

184

"Yes, Arthur killed him."

"Wayne said Arthur had issues with your family. Those issues must have been pretty bad."

"It's a long story, but in a nutshell he did it to avenge his granddaughter. She committed suicide after my dad ended their relationship."

"Why didn't your family step in to help her?"

"No one knew about the affair. Arthur said she was pregnant. Dad dumped her when she refused to have an abortion. That's when she killed herself. He wasn't worth that girl's life."

"Love doesn't always bring happy-ever after endings. I tried to pretend you were alive every time I saw a man that resembled you."

"I'm here now."

"You were dead. I couldn't bear that. I hated you for dying, and then I hated myself even more for blaming you." The words rushed out seconds before she began to cry.

Erik enfolded her in his arms and held her close. She pressed her face into his chest dampening his shirt. "Your tears are my tears now, but I hate that I made you cry."

She shook her head, exhausted by her weeping.

"It's not your fault. All I seem to do is cry these days."

Erik pulled his handkerchief out of his pants pocket and wiped the cloth over her wet lashes and cheeks. "I hope whatever tears you shed from now on will be only because you're happy."

"I don't know what happy is anymore. How did you find me?" she muttered, sniffing into the handkerchief.

"It wasn't easy, and I prayed we wouldn't be too late, considering the way you sounded in your message to Fran. Burt called my grandfather about Wayne shooting out his tires just before I told him about you being abducted. He reasoned Wayne would probably force you to give him money. Ernest asked the bank manager to call if you showed up there drawing out a large sum of money. You left before any of us could get to you."

"I didn't want to use credit cards because I thought I would leave a trail. I never expected someone to report my actual appearance."

"The manager saw you leave with a young couple and took down their license plate number. That led us to them. They told us how they helped you."

"Isn't that unusual for a bank manager to get involved in such a personal matter?"

"ELK does a lot of business with him. He'd like to keep it that way. Some people recognized you when we showed your photo. Ernest hired someone to track you down."

"Why would your grandfather go to so much trouble?"

"Why wouldn't he, considering your involvement? His man finally traced you here after weeks of dogging your footsteps."

"I never saw anyone following me."

"He's very good at what he does."

Riley frowned, and jerked her head toward a window. "Is he outside watching right now?"

"Yes, but only because I wanted to be sure you were here before I dismissed him."

"I don't want to sound ungrateful, but I don't like the idea of someone watching me."

"I'll send him away," Erik said and made the phone call while Riley sat listening.

"I hope Ernest won't be angry with me," Riley said when Erik ended the call.

"He just wanted to make sure you were safe."

"That was very kind. Please tell him I said thank you."

"You can thank him yourself when you go back with me."

She shook her head. "I think it would be better for you and your family if I don't go back. My life there is over. I've made a new life for myself here."

He touched a fingertip to the soft skin tinged with gray beneath one eye. "We all want you to return. Fran and I are trying to figure out a way to get the money out of those offshore accounts that Wayne and Melvin set up. She'll use the one with her name on it to go to the boys' college fund and the other to Geraldine's sister. That should be good news for you."

"I hope you can work it out. I don't want you to feel bad about not coming here sooner. I'm not angry with you. I just needed to be alone."

"No one knows better than I what a person goes through when they believe they are responsible for someone's death. But you know the truth about Wayne now. He wanted payback for all the wrongs he considered we all heaped on him. You told Fran it was your fault he died. Why would you think that when the air bag caused his gun to go off?"

"How can you ask me that? Everything that happened is because of my meddling. Wayne wouldn't have been so upset if I'd left things alone. He might still be taking money from ELK, but he would be alive. You would still be living peacefully in your cabin without having to untangle the mess I made. Richard wouldn't have become suspicious if I hadn't gone to confront him in Miami. My biggest fear was the harm his thug could do to Frances and the boys."

"Another bluff. He didn't bring anyone with him. He wouldn't want to share his revenge."

She pressed fingertips to her mouth.

"Thank God, but I did put Ian and Caleb in danger."

"Not intentionally. Tanny said you called a couple of days after you left to ask if the guys were okay. You hung up before she could tell you about me."

Riley raised a brow. "You've been in touch with Tanny?"

"Yes, and she wanted me to remind you that she fell for a scheme that could have gotten her killed. But she took the chance because it involved keeping Caleb safe. She ran off without telling anyone just like you did. It's time to stop battering yourself over the decision you made, and come to grips with the fact that you did what you thought was right under the circumstances. Your friends and I all ran away at one time, but we found out that wasn't the way to solve our problems. Tessa, Ian, and Caleb agree with me."

"You've been in contact with all of them?"

Erik nodded. "They've been very concerned about you."

"I'm sorry I made them worry. It's so ironic that us three women have all had predators chasing after us. But I could have prevented mine. I traveled almost three thousand miles from Hawaii to Juneau to forget about scary times and ended up making more trouble for myself and everyone else. I don't know how to stop wishing I would have kept my nose out of your family's affairs. I'm too messed up to be any good to you or them. There's nothing you can say that will make me feel better. You can't change what's happened."

"I may not be able to alter the chain of events, but I am going to straighten you out on your logic. Your meddling as you call it not only dug up dirt, but it also dug up the truth about a lot of things. Fran knew her marriage was in trouble and it was only a matter of time before the truth came out along with Wayne's stealing. As for me living peacefully in my cabin, you know very well I was miserable. I would still be carrying around the burden of believing I was responsible for Geraldine Melvin's death if you hadn't discovered what really happened."

"What about Ian and Caleb and how I put their lives at risk by having them go to the cabin with me?"

"You needed help; and they were happy to be there for you, because you proved in the past how you were there for them in their time of need. And while you're so busy berating yourself, you've forgotten how you forced Richard Melvin out into the open. You gave Jackie a chance to avenge her sister. You discovered those offshore accounts that can now be put to good use."

"But you could have died when all those bullets starting flying."

"Yes, but you are forgetting that I happened to be at the cabin because I went to help a friend. You had nothing to do with Arthur's thirst for revenge. Wayne used that to lure me there for his own purpose, and Arthur wanted me there to see how he killed my father. Arthur also confessed that he tampered with my plane, so I would crash. That was his idea and his alone."

Riley's mouth gaped open. "Why did he want you to die when it was your father he hated?"

"He thought my being dead would make my father grieve. But it didn't take Arthur long to realize my death didn't bring the reaction he wanted. If anything, it might actually put more money in Dad's pockets with my grandfather having one less heir dipping into the inheritance."

"There are all kinds of monsters in this world. It's sad to think one of them was your father. I've been sitting here all these weeks living in limbo, filled with self-loathing while you've been having to deal with so much sadness. Makes me feel ashamed of myself."

"Don't. You've done enough of that. You made some mistakes, Riley. We all did. But continuing to blame yourself for every bad thing you think you did isn't going to help any of us now. I want you to start focusing about how much good you did for my family."

"I just don't want to screw up again after what I've done in the past."

"I'm more interested in the future. You helped to set my family free. I'm sorry it came at such a cost to you. I'm asking you to give me a chance to make up for what you've suffered."

She pointed to herself.

"I've changed. I'm no longer the person you need."

"You are exactly what I need. I've never loved a woman as much as I love you. Remember how you once said you needed me, and you believed I needed you. You were right. Your love healed me. Will you let my love heal you?"

"I'm a whiny baby, but if you want me, then you'll have to take me as I am."

"I'll take you any way I can get you." He pulled her into his arms. "Where's the bedroom?"

"That way," Riley pointed, locking her hands behind his neck when he lifted her.

He set her down next to the bed and began to undress her taking great care, stopping to kiss her after removing each article of clothing. Emotion clogged his heart and mind when he saw how thin she'd become since they'd last made love.

He lifted her on the bed and undressed himself before joining her. Early evening shadows began to filter in through the windows now dimming the room. Riley reached over and turned on a bedside lamp.

190

"I don't like the dark."

"Neither do I," Erik said and pulled her into his arms. "It's time to put all the bad things from the past behind us starting at this very moment."

"That's good advice."

Good advice . . . unless you were a person obsessed with holding onto the past and would do anything to get restitution for a wrong you believed had been committed.

Chapter Nineteen

Erik awoke during the night with the feel of Riley's legs churning against him as though she was running. But it was her weeping that had the most impact. He held her close when she called out his name begging him to wait for her. He coaxed her awake with slow, gentle strokes, whispering her name.

"I've got you. Everything is all right."

"Wayne, he's coming for me," she whimpered.

"Wayne is gone. He can't hurt you anymore. Go back to sleep. I'll be here when you wake."

Erik waited until morning to make love to Riley. He took his time. It wasn't easy keeping his own desire in check, but it was more important that she would be able to feel the full measure of whatever relief he could give to her. The sound of her weeping and the terror in her voice still rang in his ears. He needed to replace those emotions with something more pleasant.

He knew he couldn't erase the weeks of suffering by just this one time in bed, but he hoped it would be a beginning. He wanted to hear her laugh again. Erik figured he'd made a good start when Riley practically purred with satisfaction. She sat up minutes later and stretched.

"I feel wonderful! Do you want to know what I'd like to do right now?"

"Make me purr?" Erik teased.

"More like make you roar but hold that thought for later. I want to cook breakfast and serve it in bed. I can't remember the last time I've felt so hungry."

"Okay, go and cook, but promise we get to be naked when we eat."

"Absolutely." Riley scooted out of bed and began to dress. "What would you like to eat, or should I surprise you?"

"I don't mind surprises as long as they're good ones. I'll leave that up to you."

"I have to go to the store because I don't have any food in the house."

He pointed to her.

"That explains a lot."

She looked down at herself and wrinkled her nose. "I know. It's a wonder my skinny body didn't turn you off."

"It takes more than a body to make a man love a woman."

"So diplomatic. I assume you have a car here."

"Yes. I rented it at the airport. The keys are in the pocket of my pants. Take whatever money you need for food out of my wallet."

"I have my own money."

Riley finished dressing, took the keys, and blew him a kiss when she practically danced from the room. She decided to return Sally's dishes to her while she had transportation. She also couldn't wait to tell Sally how Erik showed up on the cottage doorstep yesterday.

Riley hummed as she drove. She knew where the Whites lived, although she'd never been to their house. The setting was quite picturesque situated by a lake, but a little too remote for her liking. She focused her attention on enjoying the scenery and didn't realize another car had entered the long narrow road soon after she made her own turn.

Riley gawked at the luxury homes as she drove, certain they were worth close to a million dollars or more by the looks of them. Jed and Sally's home was the original house in this area. They built their home themselves over thirty years ago before lakeside property sold at such a premium. The house stood at the very end of the road a fair distance from the closest neighbor. Real estate developers must be clamoring to get their hands on the little white bungalow with its bright blue trim. The house reminded Riley of a midget among giants as structures went.

She parked at the front of the house, picked up the bag with Sally's containers, and jogged up three steps flaked by a profusion of blooming flowers. She crossed the porch, rang the doorbell, and knocked several times without receiving any response. She would have called ahead if she hadn't been so giddy after being with Erik.

One night with him and she was practically walking on air. She could still hear his words inside her head saying she was safe now and the past was behind them. She wished she had thought to call before she drove out here. She realized she really wanted to share her good news with Sally and tell her the future was starting to look a whole lot better.

Riley set the bag on the porch and walked around to the back of the house to see if one of their vehicles was there, but the area was empty. She looked out over the lake admiring the picturesque scene. No wonder the Whites didn't want to sell. She walked to the edge of the water and smiled as a mother duck and her six fluffy ducklings swam up to her.

The sound of a vehicle approaching made her think the Whites had returned. Riley turned just as a large black sedan pulled into view and headed straight for her. She waved her arms signaling for the person to stop, but the car kept coming. Riley stood at the very edge of the lake now pinned in by two large bushes making it impossible for her to get out of the way. She spun around and cried out in pain when she felt the car bump into the back of her legs. She knew the only reason it didn't do more damage to her was because she was already toppling into water before the driver could back up and come at her again.

Riley began to shiver within seconds from the shock of the cold water and the disturbing thought that someone had deliberately tried to run her down. She had no idea who this maniac was, but they didn't appear to be in any hurry to go away. Her only avenue of escape now would be to swim until she could get out of sight from this unknown tormentor.

She hoped the person would think she had drowned if she stayed in the water long enough. Blood thundered in her ears, as she inhaled a long breath and dove deeper into the murky depths with the sound of Erik's words inside her head about no one ever hurting her again.

Someone obviously forgot to inform the person in the deadly black sedan about that.

Erik wasn't quite ready to leave the warmth of the bed and the scent of Riley's subtle body's fragrance that still lingered in the bedding. He sat up propped against the headboard with his arms crossed behind his head. He looked around the room. The walls were painted a soft cream color that complimented the dark old-fashioned furniture. Pale green curtains with a delicate pattern of rust colored leaves covered two windows. He looked down and realized the bedspread matched the curtains. Two small braided rugs lay on the pine floor by the bed.

A rather bland decor, but not necessarily uninviting. Nothing unique enough to make it distinguishable. It would be a place you could walk away from and soon forget what the house looked like. He had a feeling Riley chose it for that very reason. Erik noticed there wasn't anything personal to indicate she had lived here for weeks. No jewelry, or female clutter setting on the dresser. No framed photos. Perhaps Riley had intended this to just be a stopping off place. He wondered where she planned to go from here if he hadn't shown up. He would have to ask her, but he suspected she wouldn't have an answer.

He couldn't forget how edgy she was when he arrived and how she insisted she couldn't go back to Juneau with him. The inability to feel as though you couldn't fit in anywhere had to be particularly painful and very lonely. Nights had been the hardest for him to get through at the cabin and again when Riley ran away after Wayne's death. Nighttime wasn't any friend to her if her nightmare meant anything.

But they were together again, and Erik knew he wasn't the only one wanting to celebrate the happy occasion when he thought of Riley's offer to come back and cook breakfast. He rolled out of bed and pulled his phone out of his pants pocket. Time to call his Hawaii connection and share the good news before he headed to the bathroom for a shower.

Sally didn't recognize the black vehicle that sped by her smaller car, as she drove to her house. But she did recognize the fact that they almost forced her off the road. She planned to drive around back when she reached the house like she always did, but her foot hit the brake when she saw a car parked near the front door. Had Jed forgot to tell her he was expecting people to come calling? That would be so like him.

She grunted as she pulled herself from behind her steering wheel and peered inside the other car long enough to realize it wasn't occupied. She walked to the house and saw a bag on the porch. A quick peek revealed her containers from the food she left at Riley's. Did she buy that car outside, or maybe borrow it? If that was the case, then why wasn't she anywhere in sight?

Sally unlocked the front door, carried the bag inside, and set it along with her purse on a table. Maybe Riley had someone drive her here and they were waiting by the lake for either her or Jed to return. She walked back outside again. Sally didn't see anyone, but she did see tire tracks and followed them to the edge of the water. The tracks stopped, but closer inspection revealed footprints stamped in the soft mud before they disappeared at the water's edge.

What happened here?

Riley left the containers, but Riley wasn't in sight and an empty car was parked in the yard. Sally didn't need more evidence to have her rushing back to the house to call Riley's number. No answer. Little panting breaths huffed between her lips as she called Jed next. She knew he was in town picking up some supplies to do some repairs on their porch. He answered on the third ring.

"I want you to go to the cottage and see if Riley is home and call me as soon as you know," she said, the words tumbling out of her mouth.

"Sal, I've got a cart load of stuff I was just getting ready to go pay for. Tell Riley I'll stop by later if this is about another leaky pipe at the cottage."

"This is not about a leaky pipe. I don't have time to explain, but I think something has happened to her."

Jed's radar instantly went on full alert and all thoughts of repairing a porch became the furthest thing from his mind. He'd been married to Sally long enough to know that tone meant something had upset her and it would be better do what she said and ask questions later.

"Okay, I'm on my way."

He didn't waste another second before leaving the items in the cart and walking briskly outo his truck. It took fifteen minutes to get to the cottage. His nerves were a little jangled by the time he stood knocking on Riley's door and his heart was beating a little too hard when she didn't answer after several loud knocks. Jed stood there wondering if he would be making a fool of himself by walking into the cottage without being invited. Sally's anxious voice couldn't be denied. But better a fool than a man with regrets.

Erik stood in the shower stall enjoying the feel of the hot water spraying over his body so much that he couldn't resist singing. The bathroom was at the back of the house and the door was closed, muffling any outside sounds. He didn't hear the front door open, and he didn't hear Jed call Riley's name.

But Jed heard Erik. He nearly stumbled in his haste to get outside and call Sally. "There's a man in the cottage taking a shower, but no Riley. Did you know? Is that why you wanted me to check on her?"

"I didn't know what was going on, but I think he may have hurt Riley."

"Now, now, let's not jump to conclusions."

"Are you trying to soothe your nerves or mine, old man?" she asked, irritated.

"Both I guess. But I still don't know what made you decide something was wrong."

"Riley told me yesterday she had a madman chasing her before she escaped to here."

"Well now, that puts the situation in a different light. Are you thinking this is the guy?"

"I don't know for sure, but he could be. Riley was here at our house, Jed. I found my food containers on the porch. There's a silver Mercedes parked in our yard with no one inside."

"Riley doesn't have a car."

"I know that, but how else did my containers get here? That's not the only thing worrying me. A large black sedan practically ran me off our road when I came home. I was so busy steering I didn't see who was driving, but I bet the man in the cottage was in that car. He must have followed Riley here, did something awful to her, and went back to the cottage to clean up."

"There isn't a black sedan, or any other vehicle parked in the driveway. I can't see a black car anywhere near the house, either."

"Maybe he hid the car someplace else and walked back to the cottage, but that still doesn't explain why the other car is here."

"This all sounds pretty drastic, Sal." Jed tilted his ballcap back and scratched his bald head. "Are you sure you aren't mistaken? This guy could just be a friend visiting her."

"Have you ever heard Riley say she's made any friends since she moved here?"

"No, but that doesn't mean she hasn't. We can't expect her to tell us everything."

"I realize that, but I found tire tracks leading to the edge of the lake and footprints."

Jed inhaled a sharp breath. "Are you saying someone drove a car into the water?"

"No. I'm concerned about the footprints. I'm going to go back and take a closer look."

"Maybe we should call the police."

"That could take too long, and Riley might not have a lot of time. I don't want you to put yourself in danger, but you need to find out who her mysterious visitor is."

"Okay, I'll think of something."

Chapter Twenty

Erik expected to see Riley when he walked into the bedroom . . . not a man pointing a hunting rifle at him. A quick flashback of Arthur and his gun made Erik grit his teeth. He was getting sick and tired of people threatening him. But more importantly, he was sick with worry wondering if Riley was all right. He had no idea what this guy wanted, but it obviously wasn't a social call. Did this gun toting grandpa come here looking for her?

"Mind telling me why you're pointing that gun at me?" Erik asked, masking his concern

Jed lifted the gun higher.

"What have you done with Riley?"

"I haven't done anything with her. She went to the store to buy some breakfast food."

"Why?"

Erik couldn't believe how ridiculous this conversation sounded.

"Because she was hungry."

"Don't get smart with me, fella."

"I'm not trying to get smart with you. Why would I when you're the one with the gun? I appreciate knowing you care about Riley. I'm also a friend of hers. I flew in from Juneau yesterday. I don't think it will take much imagination on your part to realize I spent the night here. When I said I'm a friend, I meant a very good friend."

"Did you by any chance rent a car?"

"I did, but it's not here because Riley borrowed it."

"What color is the car?"

Erik sighed irritably, his patience starting to wear thin now. "Silver."

"Not black, then," Jed muttered.

"I don't know what difference the color of my car means to you and I don't know what this is all about. But if you contact Riley, she can set things straight about me. You're not the only one who is concerned. I thought she would be back by now. Is the store very far from here?"

Jed ignored the question.

"My wife already called, and Riley's not answering. There's a silver Mercedes parked at our house. That the car you rented?"

"Yes. I told you she borrowed it to do the shopping, but she never said anything about making another stop. Are you sure it's the same car? Why would she go to your house?"

"Riley was there all right. She left some things on our porch, but my wife can't find her."

"Look, whoever you are, you're putting me on edge. Do you suspect something has happened to Riley? Because if that's the case, then I need you to take me to your house and let me search for her. I don't make my request lightly. Riley had a very bad experience before she came here, and it caused her a great deal of trauma. That's why she wanted to get away."

Jed lifted a bushy brow.

"If what you say is true, then why are you wanting to take her back?"

"Riley didn't realize it's safe to return until I came here and told her."

"My wife said something about Riley having a problem. How do I know you aren't the reason for that problem?" Jed asked, accusation filling his eyes and words.

"Well, I'm not. I don't have time to go into all the sordid details on what happened back in Juneau, but Riley thought she was protecting my family by keeping her distance. I happen to be in love with her and I came to take her home. Now either you help me or get out of my way because I'm not going to stand here without doing everything I can to find out if she's all right."

Erik took the chance and moved toward the chair where he'd thrown his clothes the night before. He let the towel slip from his hips and began to drag on his clothes silently praying this man would help him find Riley. He was afraid she wouldn't be able to survive another assault before she completely lost her mind.

And this time any amount of loving might not be enough to bring her back

Riley stayed close to the shore and swam as far as her strength would take her. She hadn't realized how out of condition she was from her lack of good nutrition and sleepless nights. She ended up gasping for air when she finally poked her head out of water keeping hidden among some foliage growing close to the shore. She didn't see the black car.

Time to find out if it would be safe to get back on shore.

She dragged herself out of the water on limbs feeling like noodles and lay on the ground panting like a dying fish fighting for its last breath. She shivered in her wet clothing that stuck to her like icy wrappings. Riley knew she had to get moving, but her body didn't seem to want to cooperate. Her mind, however, became quite active by tormenting her with the realization that someone had just tried to kill her. Who could that person be? And would they try again?

The mere thought scared her to the very marrow of her bones.

She began to believe she was safe here believing the past couldn't catch up to her. But she obviously was wrong, and she was going to have the bruises to prove it. Just how far was she going to have to go before she would ever feel safe again, she wondered? Maybe there wasn't ever going to be such a place. Her life hadn't exactly been that great lately, but that didn't mean she was anxious to hasten her demise, especially now that Erik had come to her very much alive.

Erik! Riley dug her hands into the ground filling her nails with mud, as she struggled to sit up. She had to get back to the cottage and tell him what happened. She rolled to her knees and grabbed the grass to slowly pull her body until she stood on both feet. But the sound of plodding footsteps and someone panting had her nerves jingling like loose change in a piggybank.

Riley dropped back down to the ground and lay peering through the long blades of grass while keeping her senses focused on the approaching sound. The footsteps came closer making Riley's heartbeat increase rapidly. Her teeth clamped down on trembling lips silencing the frightened scream that wanted to rise in her throat. Was it someone taking a walk along the lake?

Or the crazy person from the big black car coming back to finish the job?

Jed's phone rang. He took it out of his pocket and glanced at the screen.

"It's my wife."

Erik did up the last button on his shirt and looked at Jed.

"I hope it's good news."

Jed talked less than a minute before ending the connection. "She says I need to get back to the house right away."

"Is Riley okay?"

"Yes and no."

"What the hell does that mean?" Erik demanded to know, his entire body on alert.

"It means we have to get back to my house."

Jed barely had a chance to bring his truck to a stop before Erik was out of the cab and running to the front door. Sally heard his heavy footsteps on the porch and opened the door, thinking it would be Jed. She staggered back when Erik burst into the room.

"Where is she?"

"Who is this man?" Sally wanted to know, as soon as Jed hurried into the house.

"He says he's from Juneau and he's in love with Riley."

Sally's eyes narrowed.

"Are you Erik?"

"Yes, and I'm assuming you know that because Riley mentioned me. Is she here or not?"

"She's taking a hot bath. She jumped into the lake and was chilled to the bone when I found her. I'll tell her you're here. Go into the kitchen with Jed and have a cup of coffee."

Erik's lips tightened.

"I don't need a cup of coffee. What I need is to see Riley for myself."

"Well, you will just have to wait. I told you she's taking a bath."

"I'm sorry to shock your sensibilities, but I have seen her naked." He looked around. "Now are you going to show me where the bathroom is, or do I have to search the house on my own?"

Sally started to sputter a protest, but Jed interrupted.

"It's down the hall, third door on the left," he said, pointing.

Erik didn't waste another minute listening to Sally demanding that he stop. She watched him rush away before she put her hands on her hips and glared at Jed with enough temper to make him retreat to the kitchen with Sally right behind him. He was pretty darn sure he was going to need that coffee before she could begin to unleash her anger on him

"How could you just let him walk away without stopping him? What is that poor girl going to think when he walks in on her? Have you lost all sense of what modesty means?"

"Sal, things have changed from when we were first going together. You heard the man say he's seen her without her clothes. Young people today don't wait for the walk down the aisle before they give themselves to each other. They're lovers and if you doubt his feeling for Riley, then you didn't take a very good look at his expression. They have a right to some privacy without having us sticking our noses into their personal business."

"I'll wait, but I don't have to like it. He didn't even give me a chance to explain why Riley jumped into the lake."

"That's why we're going to let her tell him everything on her own. Now let's have some coffee while we wait. I sure would like to know myself why she ended up in the water. Maybe you can tell me how you found her. You were really scared when you called me, Sal. What's going on with Riley?"

Erik eased the bathroom door open. Riley's eyes were closed, as she lay with her head leaning back against the rim of the tub. Someone had poured bubble bath into the water filling the room with a floral fragrance. He hoped the warm water was helping her to relax. Something traumatic must have happened to make her think she had to jump into the lake knowing how cold that water would be. A chill of goosebumps spread over his own arms. How many more times was Riley going to be in put in a dangerous situation? When was she ever going to get a break?

"Riley?" he said, keeping his voice low. She opened her eyes and looked at him.

"You found me . . . again. I didn't run away this time. Honest."

"I'm glad to hear it. Who are these people?"

"My landlords. How did you meet them?"

"The old man came charging into the cottage demanding to know what I did to you. Now I find out you took a swim in the lake. Kind of cold for that, don't you think?"

"Freezing, and I didn't go into the water by choice, believe me. It was the only way I could get away. Someone tried to run me down in their car. They drove right at me, so I had to jump into the water to save myself."

"What!" The word burst out of Erik.

"My God. Were you able to get a look at the driver?"

"It was kind of difficult because I was busy trying to get out of the way, but I did catch a glimpse through the windshield of a woman with platinum colored hair."

"Platinum hair?" Erik's body stiffened for a moment and he quickly looked away before Riley could see his infuriated expression.

"I don't know anyone here except Jed and Sally," she said, making Erik face her again.

"So, you've never seen this woman before?"

"No. I can't understand why she went after me. I asked Sally if she knew a woman who looked like that, but she didn't. Maybe the lady was drunk or on drugs and turned down their road by mistake. She may not even realize what she was doing when she tried to run me down. She could even be mentally ill and thought I was someone else entirely."

Erik wouldn't share his thoughts with Riley until he could be sure of his suspicions, but he was afraid the past may have caught up with them after all. The urge to shake his fists in the air raging at the injustice of it all rose strong in him. How many times were they going to come close to dying before they would be allowed to go on living?

Thinking of their problems made Erik remember all the terrible things he knew Ian and Tessa and Caleb and Tanny had been forced to endure before they were finally able to find some peaceful stability in their lives. He felt as though they belonged to a unique club where few people were meant to join, and fewer were meant to survive.

They survived, but the dues had come at a high cost.

Riley had just survived the latest battle, but the war wasn't over yet.

Another, unexpected enemy had emerged, and they clearly had murder on their mind.

Chapter Twenty-one

"I'm sure you're probably right about the woman being intoxicated and you just happened to be in the wrong place at the wrong time."

"Story of my life." She blew a handful of bubbles into the air.

"Are we having fun yet?"

Erik's mouth tilted in a lopsided grin, appreciating her attempt at humor.

"I don't blame you for feeling fed up, considering all the hell you've been through. You know, it just occurred to me that you would be better off not to come back to Juneau with me right away after all."

Riley wiggled wet fingers in her ears.

"Did I hear you correctly? Last night you couldn't wait to take me with you. I was just getting used to that idea and the more you talked about it the more I liked it. I don't want to stay here now that I know we can be together again, Erik. You showed up on my doorstep and a dream came true for me."

"I didn't mean for you to stay here. Tessa and Tanny begged me to ask you to spend some time with them. It would be selfish of me to deny them that. They've missed you very much."

"I've missed them, too, but I'm kind of embarrassed to show up at their homes after weeks of ignoring them. What kind of a friend does that make me?"

"A very confused one at the time. I called them this morning and explained everything."

"What did they say?"

"I think Caleb summed it up nicely and I quote, 'Tell her to get her butt over here right now'. The others were a little less eloquent but shared the same sentiment."

"It's nice to be wanted."

"I was so anxious to take you with me I failed to think how you would benefit more by spending some time with them first. It will help you to get used to the idea of going back to a place you felt you had to escape. It's going to be tough letting you go to Hawaii, but as it happens, I just found out I have some unexpected business to take care of that came up at home."

"Can't you do it via phone?"

Erik shook his head.

"I need to be there in person."

"Promise me you won't take too long."

"You can bet on it. I will come to you as quickly as I can. I'm looking forward to making love to you on a tropical beach."

"Hmmm, that sounds nice."

"It will be. Now I think it's time you got out of the tub," he said, dipping his hand in the cooling water. He shook out the bath towel Sally left on a stool and reached a hand to Riley.

"You're right. My body is starting to look like a prune," she said, taking his hand.

Erik wrapped the towel around her. "I should warn you that your landlady was quite shocked to know I intended on coming in here while you were naked. She's probably going to think I took advantage of you while we've been in here."

"You can take advantage of me any time you'd like."

"How about we wait until we get back to the cottage?" he suggested when Riley rubbed her body against him. "Otherwise, I'm afraid your friend might end up coming after me with a rolling pin."

Riley rested against Erik's chest.

"I wanted to die when I thought I'd lost you. I couldn't wrap my head around the idea of ever loving anyone again as much as I loved you. I feel like you are sharing not only your body, but your very soul with me when we make love."

"If I share my soul with you it's only half of what I feel you give to me in return," he said, kissing her lips rosy from their lovemaking. "I believe I fell in love with you that first night I held you in my arms after finding you in the storm. I knew it was more than physical attraction after spending those days with you in the cabin. I made the difficult decision to let you go because I wasn't the right man for you then. It took every bit of my willpower to leave, but I was determined not to ask you to accept me until I could prove to both of us that I would be worthy."

"Being alone here with you in the cottage reminds me of our time in your cabin." She smiled. "You know, I just remembered I owe you a breakfast."

"Yes, you do, but you've been rather busy."

"How do you like your eggs?"

"Any way you care to prepare them, but this time I'm going to the store with you."

Riley wrinkled her nose.

"Afraid I might get into trouble again?"

"The thought had crossed my mind."

Ian, in his never-ending ability to make things happen arranged for Riley to fly in a friend's private plane to the island once Erik called and told Tessa Riley would be coming for a visit. Jed and Sally hugged her and wished her well, waving away her apology for leaving them with such short notice. Experience with their own sorrow made them only too happy to see Riley be given a chance to have a better future for herself.

She had a wonderful time catching up with her friends while they all waited impatiently for Erik to join them. That would make their circle of six complete. But Erik had good reason to delay that reunion. He never mentioned what business he had that was so important it needed his personal attention because he knew it would be far too disturbing for Riley.

He was upset enough himself. Erik had a pretty good idea who tried to run Riley down when she described the woman. It didn't take him long to find out his theory was right once he arrived back home and confronted the person. The mysterious woman was none other than Harper, his father's last girlfriend. Riley didn't recognize her because Harper dyed her hair after Riley left.

Erik summoned her to his office and confronted her.

"I will have you brought up on charges of attempted murder if you ever go near Riley again," he bit out each word without bothering to disguise the rage he felt.

Harper clutched her throat.

"What are you talking about? I haven't seen her in ages."

"No? Then you deny driving a black sedan at her until you forced her into a lake?"

Her brightly painted red lips lifted in a superior smirk.

"You should be more careful before you make false accusations. I don't own a black sedan and I've never been to Washington, so it wasn't me who tried to hurt your precious Riley. I could sue you for trying to ruin my reputation, but I'll let it go if you agree to give me the money your father would have wanted me to have as part of his inheritance."

"I never mentioned anything about Riley being in Washington," Erik said in a calm voice.

"Everyone here knows that's where she's been," she said after a quick moment of barely concealed panic.

"No. The only people who knew was myself, my grandfather, and the man he hired to track her down. We only discovered her whereabouts recently ourselves. I'm interested to know how you found out and how long you've been planning to go after Riley."

Harper jerked out of her chair.

"I don't have to sit here and take this from you!"

She started to storm to the door until Erik's next words made her freeze.

"I have proof, including a copy of the contract for the car you rented. The woman who lives in the lake house watched from her window and saw you force Riley into the lake." Sally wasn't a witness, but Harper didn't need to know that.

"Care to change your story?"

Harper sank back down onto the chair.

"I just wanted my money, and I would have had it if Riley hadn't turned you all against me."

"We both know that's a lie. I want to know how you found Riley."

She took a handkerchief out of her purse and dabbed at her damp upper lip.

"I knew Riley disappeared after Edward and Wayne's deaths. It was no secret here in the office that she was your lover so I kept my eye out for you, using my grief over your father to come here. My big break came one day when I happened to be in a hallway and overheard you talking on the phone with Ernest about a detective locating Riley in Blaine, Washington."

She wiped her mouth again.

"May I have some water, please?"

Erik got up, went to a mini fridge, and yanked out a bottle. He loosened the cap and handed it to her. Harper raised the bottle to her lips and drank deeply. Erik returned to sit behind his desk again.

"You were saying?"

"Instinct told me you would be wanting to get to Riley, so I made plane reservations to Blaine and waited at the airport until I saw you when you arrived. I already had the car and followed you to the cottage. I saw Riley come to her door and faint when she saw you. I spent the night in my car until I followed Riley the next morning to that house by the lake."

Erik picked up a gold pen lying on the desk and began to tap it on the surface. Harper's eyes watched the motion like a cobra eyeing a swaying flute.

"What did you do after Riley disappeared into the water?"

"I waited to see if she would surface and left when there wasn't any sign of her. I drove to her house in case I was wrong about her drowning. I saw you when you two came back, so I decided to come home and . . ."

"Have another chance at her," Erik ground out, tossing the pen down.

Harper needed another drink badly, but her hand trembled so much she ended up spilling more water down the front of her blouse than getting the liquid into her mouth when she watched Erik's facial muscles twist into a mask of rage.

"Listen very carefully because I will only say this once. You will leave Juneau today. I don't care where you go, but if I ever hear of you contacting Riley or anyone in my family either by yourself or via a proxy, I will have you locked away for a very long time. Is that clear?"

Clear enough that Harper scrambled out of her chair and dropped her water bottle in her haste to scurry to the door. Erik bolted out of his own chair before she could flee the room. She shrank away from him and covered her head with her arms as though she may be expecting a blow. This time she dropped her purse onto the floor. Erik picked it up and shoved the bag back at her forcing her to grab a hold of it.

"I asked you if I made myself clear."

"Yes!" she cried, fighting panic that rose within her. "Now please let me get out of here."

He yanked open the door and bowed to Harper with a flourish. "With pleasure."

Erik waited a few days after Harper left making sure she didn't try to sneak back. Ernest promised to have her apartment watched just to make sure after Erik flew to Oahu. Erik didn't have any intention to inform Riley about his meeting with Harper. Better to let her think the person in the black car was under the influence of alcohol or drugs. A case of mistaken identity was a lot better than knowing someone had deliberately set out to murder you.

They'd both been there and done that before. It was time to scrape the layers of that kind of terror off their backs. He didn't want to do anything that would spoil their time together. Erik decided to let her make the decision when she felt ready to return to Juneau. He hoped being with her most trusted friends would be enough for her to regain her emotional and physical health.

But he knew something still wasn't quite right as the days passed. Riley often woke up during the night crying and leaving Erik feeling helpless as he tried to calm her. She seemed to suffer what appeared to be bouts of sadness even in the middle of being with her friends on what should be happy occasions. He became even more worried when Riley went off on her own, sometimes for hours at a time.

Erik's concern grew until he couldn't resist asking Tessa and Tanny what they thought he should do. They agreed that something was still bothering Riley and suggested Erik try to coax her into sharing what it was. He hinted he thought Riley might feel more comfortable sharing her feelings with them. But they believed it was more important that he be the one to break through her wall of silence to help solidify his relationship with Riley.

Erik took their advice to heart even though he didn't know how he was going to handle the situation. The problem was how to approach Riley without making the predicament worse and end up driving a wedge between them that would ruin their chance for future happiness. His opportunity came a few days after his conversation with Tessa and Tanny.

Erik and Riley were taking a day to themselves with a drive around the island. He stopped at a little store on their route and bought a couple sandwiches and soft drinks. He found a picnic table in a quiet area that Tessa told him about. Erik waited until they finished eating before he approached the subject that weighed so heavily on his mind.

"Nice view here," he said, keeping the tone of his voice casual.

"Yes, it really is lovely. I didn't even know it was here. Did you just happen to find it by accident?"

"No. Tessa told me she thought it was a good spot."

"You wouldn't think to find this kind of solitude on such a busy island. There's a kind of peacefulness here. I'm glad you brought me."

"So am I." Erik took a hold of Riley's hand. "Are you feeling at peace now?"

"Yes. Why do you ask?"

"I think you already know the answer to that," he said as gently as he could. She started to pull her hand away, but he held on.

"Talk to me, Riley."

"We are talking."

"You said you were at peace a moment ago, but that's not how you feel right now, is it?"

"Well, what do you expect after your comment?"

"I understand why you are probably feeling resentful that I just ruined what started out as a good day, but we both know something's been bothering you. I love you and I know you love me . . . or have your feelings changed toward me?"

Riley jerked her hand again and this time Erik allowed her to pull free. "You know I love you. I don't understand why you would even think otherwise."

"I guess I just need you to set me straight on a few things. Do you remember the night you found me in my office, and I ended up telling you everything that was bothering me?"

"Yes, I do and look where that got me."

"We are not going back through all of that again. I brought that night up because I wanted to remind you how we both agreed there would be no more games between us. Trust and truth, Riley. I need that from you now. Our future relationship depends on it. I think you know that, but you just haven't been able to put into words what's been bothering you."

"What makes you think something is bothering me?" she asked, wariness entering her voice.

"This conversation can't have any merit if you keep answering my questions with questions of your own. You want me to spell out why I'm concerned, then I will. You are waking up at night crying, and nothing I do helps. I see a sadness about you even when everyone else is trying to make you happy. I wonder if you even realize that, or how you've been going off on your own more and more and staying away a little bit longer each time. I'm not the only one seeing this. Your friends have also noticed how you are shutting us all out."

"I'm sorry. I didn't mean to be a problem."

He exhaled, fighting frustration.

"Riley, the only problem is you not telling any of us what's troubling you. There's no shame in asking for help. I know what closing yourself off from others can do to a person. I did it for too long and it was like living a half-life."

Riley swung her legs over the bench and walked a few feet away, keeping her back to Erik. She stood by a low stone wall staring at the valley below. She saw a couple cows munching on grass and several birds flying around, small dots in the brilliant sky. She reached down and plucked a flowering weed growing by her feet, crushing the buds between her agitated fingers.

"If you must know, I'm being hounded by guilt. I realize you said I shouldn't blame myself for what happened to your family. I've been working on that and most of the time I feel as though I'm doing better getting over those feelings. But now I find myself struggling with a whole new set of reasons to worry. Your idea to have me come back here to be with my friends sounded great at the time and I have enjoyed being with them."

"Has something happened to change that?"

Riley turned to face him. "I drove by Dad's bakery, only it isn't his anymore. I keep asking myself how I could have sold it knowing how much that place meant to him. I gave his boat to a friend, but even that somehow seems wrong. As if that wasn't enough, I've been feeling guilty I caused my mother to die. I messed up your family's lives, and I messed up my parents' lives."

Erik rose and walked over to her. "You have got to get over this compulsion you have for blaming yourself for things that are not your fault. I never met your parents, but I do know they produced a fantastic daughter. Your mother gave you the gift of life. What you've done with that life is your gift to her because you are a very loving, caring person. As for selling the bakery, I doubt if your father would have wanted you to keep a place that made you unhappy. It could never be the same without him being there. Every good parent wants their child to spread their wings and seek their own future."

"If that's true, then why am I thinking about these things?"

"I'm no expert, but perhaps the guilt you felt over what happened in Juneau unlocked some feelings you didn't realize you were harboring. I believe in time we can work this out."

"How? I've built this wall around me and cemented it in place with mortar made of guilt. How do you tear something like that down?"

"Brick by brick." Erik stepped over bringing himself close enough to cup her face between his hands. "We are going to rip into that mortar until it's reduced to nothing more than fine grains of sand, but we have to do it together."

She leaned her head on his shoulder.

"I can live with that as long as I have your help."

Chapter Twenty-two

Riley pressed both palms against her cheeks in a vain effort to control her jumpy pulse. She couldn't help being nervous at the thought of seeing Frances, despite Erik assuring her his sister was looking forward to this visit. She had missed seeing Frances all the months she'd been away, but their relationship would be different now. Riley appreciated the letter from Frances saying she forgave her for any wrongdoing in Wayne's death, but would they be able to ignore all the other bad things?

It was one thing to read a letter and another thing entirely to see the person face to face.

Erik arranged for the meeting to take place at the family home. Frances met Riley at the front door and immediately hugged her.

"We have the house to ourselves. I thought we could have coffee in the sunroom. I hope that's all right."

"That's fine, but I hope you didn't go to a lot of trouble."

Frances smiled.

"I didn't. I know you're nervous, Riley, but you needn't be."

She followed Frances to the back of the house where a small round table sat with delicate looking china cups and saucers, a carafe, and an assortment of petits fours on a plate edged with pink roses. A pink cloth and linen napkins sprinkled with a pattern of rose petals to match the china lay by the two place settings.

"It's lovely, Frances, but you didn't have to do all this just for me."

"I bet you didn't know I have a thing about roses," Frances said, ignoring the comment before waving Riley to one of the chairs.

Riley sat down, reached into her purse, drew out a small giftwrapped box, and handed it to Frances. "I brought you something."

"Thank you, but you know you didn't have to come bearing gifts. Shall I open it now, or would you rather wait until we have our coffee?"

"I'd like you to open it now."

"I was hoping you'd say that," Frances smiled, tore away the paper, and opened the box. She held up a bracelet with its gold chain and small green turtle charm. "It's lovely."

"I'm glad you like it."

"Does the charm have a special significance?"

"Yes. Hawaii Green Sea Turtles symbolize good luck, endurance, long life, wisdom, and patience. When lost, turtles are excellent navigators and often find their way home."

"What a wonderful story."

"My friends Tessa and Tanny bought me one just before I left." Riley pulled back the sleeve of her sweater to show her own bracelet. "I did know about the sea turtle story from growing up in Hawaii, but I haven't thought about it for years. I believe it symbolizes all the things you and I could use in our lives right now."

"I couldn't agree more." Frances stretched her arm across the table and handed the bracelet to Riley. "Will you do the honors?"

Riley clipped the chain around Frances's wrist with fingers that weren't quite steady. Frances squeezed her hands. "Everything is going to be okay, Riley. This is a new beginning."

"I hope so."

Frances picked up the plate and held it out to Riley. "Would you like a petit four?"

"I'd love one."

"Why not take two? Then I won't feel so bad when I do."

Riley laughed. "Why not?"

It didn't take long for Riley to realize Erik was right about how Frances viewed Wayne. The old saying that familiarity breeds contempt turned out to be true for him and in his case, it also brought indifference on his part. Riley could see Frances and the boys were already building a better life without Wayne. The aura of tension in the household seemed to have ebbed away leaving a much more relaxed atmosphere.

Frances shared her emotions openly with Riley. The sleepless nights. Loss of appetite. Weeks of wondering what she could have done to make things better before they got worse. She clearly had her own struggles with guilty feelings for misjudging Wayne and bringing him into her family. Her honesty helped Riley further understand her own painful journey and made her realize Erik was probably correct in his theory.

She told Frances about Sally and how that brave woman suggested Riley learn to forgive herself. That seemed to help Frances and made Riley determined to take Sally's advice. She owed it to Erik to start putting all her energy into building a future, instead of dwelling on the wreck of the past. His family was willing to try, so why shouldn't she?

Even Ernest made Riley feel good about her return in his own gruff way. She knew he wanted her to be part of his family when he invited her to join him for breakfast not long after her return. He prepared her toast himself . . . with marmalade. Riley worried he might want to talk about Wayne's death and why she stayed away so long. But much to her relief, he didn't mention any of those touchy subjects. They both shared a good laugh when he told Riley he knew he wanted her in the family after she told him she didn't grow up eating whale blubber.

Erik proposed marriage soon after they returned to Juneau. She accepted before he could even get down on one knee. Neither of them wanted to make their wedding be a media circus in town. They opted for a simple ceremony in a small chapel and a dinner reception with just family and very close friends in attendance. Erik didn't waste any time before he contracted to start having a house built for them. They stayed in her apartment while the construction was going on.

Riley was snuggling with Erik in bed one night and began to talk about their new upcoming home.

"I can't believe how quickly things are moving along with the house."

"That's because I hired extra workers, so we can take advantage of the good weather."

"I thought there seemed to be a lot of people there. I chose paint today for the interior. I hope you're going to like what I picked out."

"I trust your judgment, as long as you didn't get too wild."

"Everything will be in neutral tones except for one bedroom."

"What do you mean? Why should that particular room be a problem?"

"The thing is, I'm not sure if the room should be painted blue or pink."

She held her breath and waited. It took Erik less than ten seconds to realize the significance of what Riley was telling him.

"You're pregnant," he said with a huge grin.

"I just found out today. We made a baby, Erik."

"Oh, my love, you've made me very happy," he said, his voice hoarse with emotion.

The room needed to be painted pink to welcome the arrival of Elizabeth Lacey King. Ernest gave his blessing that a female in the family would finally be able to share his initials. Erik and Frances decided their grandfather must be getting sentimental in his advanced years because he gave in when Riley told him Elizabeth had been her own mother's name.

Ian and Tessa, Caleb and Tanny and their little ones came to visit Erik and Riley in Juneau when baby Elizabeth was three months old. Riley looked around as they all gathered in the living room of her new home. The men were standing in a circle talking sports while the women were talking about babies. Frances cuddled her niece while her sons sat by her making funny faces trying to coax a smile out of their infant cousin.

Riley glanced over at the men. Erik turned his head at the same moment and winked at her. That one small gesture filled her heart with so much love she knew she would never feel lonely again. It wasn't as if she didn't have people in her life before she met Erik. She had her father and grandparents and her wonderful friends. But she had always felt something was missing. Erik had been looking for that one special person to make him feel complete, too.

But now their search was over . . . even if she did have to almost die in a snowstorm for them to find each other.

Other Books by
Olivia Claire High

The Crystal Angel

The Rose Cottage

Dreams~ Shadows of the Night

A Stranger's Eyes

The Wolf Deception

Kari's Destiny

The Black Feather

New Beginnings

The Silent Ones

The Innocent Ones